Robin Moore

The Man with the Silver Oar

HARPERCOLLINS*PUBLISHERS*

Library of Congress Cataloging-in-Publication Data

Moore, Robin.

The man with the silver oar / by Robin Moore.

p. cm.

ISBN 0-380-97877-6 — ISBN 0-06-000048-1 (lib. bdg.)

Summary: In 1718, fifteen-year-old Daniel leaves his guardian uncle's Quaker household to stowaway on a ship in pursuit of a pirate captain bent on raiding the coast of North America before returning to port in Hispaniola.

1. Pirates—Fiction. 2. Seafaring life—Fiction. 3. Adventures and adventurers—Fiction. 4. Orphans—Fiction. 5. Quakers—Fiction. 6. Philadelphia (Pa.)—Fiction. 7. Atlantic Coast (U.S.)—Fiction. 8. Hispaniola—History—18th century—Fiction.

PZ7.M78766 Man 2002   2001042407

[Fic] 21   CIP

                                                              AC

1 2 3 4 5 6 7 8 9 10

First Edition

"Blood is thicker than water . . ."
—old folk saying

TABLE OF CONTENTS

CHAPTER ONE

❧

*D*ANIEL COLLINS had never been to a hanging before.

His uncle, a peaceful Quaker, had strictly forbidden him to attend these gruesome public spectacles. And Daniel always obeyed his uncle's wishes.

But here he was, clinging to the branches of a stout oak tree, less than fifty yards from the gallows.

It was Tuck O'Neil who first told him about the hangings.

"You really should go," Tuck always said. "It's your public duty to see the scoundrels hang. And besides," he'd say with a wink, "it's the best entertainment the streets of Philadelphia have to offer."

Tuck was no Quaker. He was a red-haired Irish brawler who knew the city streets like the back of his hand.

On the outside, Tuck and Daniel were alike in many ways. They were long and lanky, with strong backs and large, capable hands. They were both tolerably handsome and clear-eyed. They were both in their fifteenth year, eager to cast off the ties that bound them to their homes and families and ship out for the open sea.

But on the inside, the two young men were as different as

night and day. Daniel was no brawler. He had been raised in a pious Quaker household that sparkled with cleanliness and holy conversation. There was no music permitted in the house, no dancing, and certainly no talk of criminals and hangings. His Sundays were spent in the quiet meditation of Quaker Meeting, where he sat with Uncle Elias in the great holy silence, listening for the echoes of God's word.

When the other apprentices laid aside their tools and left the heat and dust of the shipyard to venture down to the execution dock, Daniel had always remained behind, secure in the knowledge that he was doing the right thing. He wanted adventure, sure enough, but he had no appetite for cruelty.

Later he would listen with downcast eyes and sweating palms as the rowdy boys described the neck-stretching in vivid detail.

He listened. But he did not laugh when they laughed. He did not make jokes. He did not gawk at their souvenirs— hanks of hair and rope and pieces of dead man's clothing. Instead, he vowed to himself that he would never take part in such savagery.

But today was different.

It was June 5, 1718. And this was no ordinary execution. Today the notorious pirates, Hatchet Jack Morgan and Moses Skellington, would be hung from the public gallows before a thousand eager spectators.

"You can't miss this, Daniel," Tuck said. "There'll be a parade and a sermon and confessions and such."

Daniel looked up from his place in the sawpit. The workday was nearly over. The sun was dipping down, casting a golden light on the water and the wharves and the hulks of the unfinished ships. A wind came up from the eastern shore, smelling cool and green.

For an instant, Daniel's mind swam with possibilities. A parade. A sermon. A last dying speech from each of the pirates. An execution. Suddenly his life seemed very small. Daniel had never seen any of these things. And he feared he never would.

"Well," Tuck said, "are you comin' or aren't you?"

"I must admit . . ." Daniel said slowly, "I would like to see a pirate."

"Who wouldn't?" Tuck said, grabbing him by the arm.

Then, before Daniel had time to say another word, Tuck had pulled him up out of the sawpit and they were walking past the sawdust piles and the weathered stacks of lumber, past the barrels of lime and the piles of gravel, up out of the shipyard, toward the waterfront docks.

Daniel had to walk fast to keep up. He didn't want to be left behind, not this time.

And here they were, in the shelter of the leafy branches, twenty feet above the heads of the crowd. The tree they had chosen was close to the gallows and close to the river, standing alone along the muddy bank. Often the waters of high tide covered her roots.

From their perch in the fork of the tree, Tuck and Daniel could see everything.

3

To the north, a covey of graceful ships lay anchored in the depth of the river channel, copper-colored in the slanting afternoon light.

To the south, the Delaware River flowed on its twisting journey, nearly seventy miles downstream from here, through fertile farmlands and piney swamps, all the way to the Atlantic Ocean.

To the east, the green banks of New Jersey shimmered in the heat.

To the west, the sober faces of the red-brick buildings and ordered streets of the Quaker city receded into the haze.

Directly ahead, a gallows had been erected on the black mud of the riverbank. Daniel had seen many wooden structures in his time, but none like this.

It was horrible in its simplicity: The framework overhead consisted of a heavy wooden beam supported by two stout timbers. From this beam, the ropes would dangle and the pirates would hang. The beam stood a good ten feet above the platform. And this platform stood like a stage a dozen feet above the level of the ground. This way, the whole crowd had a clear view of the hanging.

The cobblestone promenade surrounding the hangman's scaffold teemed with people of every description: Bankers and bootblacks, sailors and seamstresses, printers, pickpockets, and politicians all stood on tiptoe, jostling against one another as they craned their necks, each searching for a clear view of the execution site.

Somewhere a man with a cockney accent was plucking a fiddle and singing:

Hangin's the best way to die
for the poor, it's better than livin'
because when the gallows is high,
the journey is shorter to heaven . . .

Nearby a cluster of drunken men took up the tune, braying like donkeys. The laughter of their female companions was shrill, like carrion crows.

At the edge of the crowd, underneath the tree where the boys roosted, two men in red-striped shirts began selling bottles of apple cider and blackberry wine from a wooden handcart.

A dozen women, carrying huge pewter trays loaded with pastries and dried apples, moved like sailing ships through the crowd. A small army of barefoot children fanned out across the commons, hawking handbills that described the most lurid details of the pirates' lives.

Tuck pulled one from his pocket, smoothing it out on his leg.

"Here," he said to Daniel. "Cast your eyes on this."

Daniel looked down at the trampled sheet. It was printed in brown ink on cheap yellow paper.

Across the top, he could make out a bold headline:

EXECUTION OF THE PYRATES. AN ACCOUNT OF THE MURDERS AND CRUELTIES COMMITTED BY HATCHET JACK MORGAN AND MOSES SKELLINGTON, FOR WHICH THEY ARE TO SUFFER THE PAIN OF EXECUTION AT THE PUBLIC GALLOWS.

But before he could read further, he was startled by a great shout that went up from the crowd. All eyes were turned to the River Road. Like the sound of distant thunder, he could hear the rumbling of wagon wheels on cobblestones.

The carnival of death was about to begin.

A wind came up, blowing from the east across the river. Daniel clung tight to the branches.

"He's coming now," Tuck shouted, pointing with his chin. His eyes were on the River Road.

"Who?" Daniel asked.

"Look and see for yourself."

Just then, the executioner appeared, driving a flatbed wagon pulled by a pair of black stallions. Two boys, whom Daniel took to be the hangman's apprentices, bounced along in the wagon bed. The executioner was a huge man, barrel-chested and broad-shouldered, with a long beard and heavy, arching eyebrows. He was dressed entirely in black, with a wide-brimmed hat and a strange overcoat that trailed down to the tops of his boots.

The hangman drove the wagon to the edge of the execution dock and climbed down, tying his horses to a post driven into the ground. He mounted the staircase to the wooden platform. Over each shoulder, he carried a coil of heavy rope. The boys followed behind, carrying a battered wooden ladder.

Daniel watched as the boys hauled the ladder up onto the platform. They leaned it against the overhead beam, then held it steady as the big man climbed to the top rung. One by one, he tied the ropes to the beam, making sure that each was positioned over a trapdoor Daniel could see cut into the platform below. With practiced hands, he fashioned the dangling end of each rope into a noose.

The hangman pulled a lump of something from his pocket. He rubbed it over the twisted strands of rope.

Tuck leaned close to Daniel's ear.

"Beeswax," he said. "So the nooses slip like silk. Otherwise the poor fellows just hang there for a few moments and strangulate—dancing in the sheriff's picture frame, they call it."

Meanwhile the apprentices were unloading their tar buckets and brushes.

"After the pirates are cut down," Tuck explained, "they'll lay them on the street and coat their bodies with tar to keep the birds and insects away. Then the corpses will be hung in chains at the head of the harbor, in plain view of every passing ship—I suppose that would make you think twice about going a-pirating, wouldn't it?"

Daniel didn't answer. He had a sinking feeling in the pit of his stomach. This was no theater play. This was for real.

Suddenly the crowd began to cheer.

"There's the execution procession," Tuck said, nodding toward a column of men marching down the River Road.

A solitary man, dressed in a blood-red waistcoat and a white powdered wig, walked twenty paces ahead of the others. As he came closer, Daniel could see that he carried a long oar, painted silver and inscribed with many curious symbols. He held it high, so all could see.

"That's The Man with the Silver Oar," Tuck said. "The Silver Oar is the sign of a pirate execution. It is the token of authority of the Lord High Admiral in London. You can see the gallows are not erected on dry land, but on the river bank, in between the high and low tide marks, to show that this is a crime of the sea. The legends say that one out of every thirteen pirates dies on the gallows. And when a pirate's end is near, he will often say that the Man with the Silver Oar has come for him at last."

So, Daniel thought, this is Death Himself, elegantly dressed in a waistcoat and powdered wig, with red ribbons fluttering in the wind.

Behind the oarsman, a formation of red-coated British regulars walked in lockstep, with feathered hats, shiny boots, and muskets at their shoulders. Following them were the dark ranks of the Anglican priests, stoop-shouldered in their black coats, clutching their Bibles to their chests, looking for all the world like a flock of hungry vultures.

And behind them, barefoot and in chains, were the pirates themselves.

When the crowd caught sight of the sea rovers, a thunderous roar again filled the commons. Tuck roared too, raising both fists into the air.

Daniel had never seen a pirate before. And here were two of them, in broad daylight, less than fifty yards away.

As they mounted the platform, Daniel devoured them with his eyes, feasting on their misery.

Hatchet Jack was a small, angular man with a face like a weapon, sharp-edged and cruel. His eyes were small and black as coal tar. His thin gray hair was pulled back into a tight braid. Dressed in baggy blue seaman's trousers and a ragged red shirt with billowing sleeves, he moved quickly, twitching and licking his lips, like a rabbit caught in a trap.

Like his companion, Moses Skellington was dressed in colorful rags. But Skellington was an entirely different creature. He was tall and powerfully built, a man in his prime, with hair that hung long down his back, shining blue-black, like a crow's wing. His eyes danced with a strange, almost primitive light. On his chin was the hint of a wispy beard. The corners of his mouth were upturned slightly, as if he were amused by all of the excitement.

Daniel watched as two soldiers led the pirates to their places on the execution stage.

"How does it work?" Daniel asked.

Tuck grinned.

"Gravity."

"No, really, how does it work?"

Tuck sighed. He pretended to be annoyed, but Daniel could see that he was clearly enjoying his role as the execution guide.

"See those two taut cords tied to the beam at the back of the platform?" Tuck asked.

Daniel nodded.

"Each one is stretched tight across the platform and holds a trapdoor in place. The hangman cuts the cord, the trap falls away, and the pirate drops. Or at least that's how it's supposed to work. Things do not always go so smoothly. Execution is an imperfect science, you know."

Daniel was still thinking that over as the hangman slipped the stiffened nooses over the pirates' heads and snugged them tight.

A handsome naval officer with an ornate sword at his belt stepped forward and, producing a small key, unlocked the chains that encircled the pirates' ankles and wrists. Two soldiers dragged the chains away. The hangman bound the criminals' wrists before them with tight cords. The officer looked at each condemned man's face, then turned on his heel and descended the stairs, taking his place among the military ranks.

A tall, somber-faced clergyman mounted the platform and raised his right hand. As if this were a play that had been rehearsed many times, the crowd fell silent.

"Let us pray." the minister murmured, removing his black-brimmed hat.

A thousand heads were uncovered and bowed in the sunlight. It was a long prayer, mostly inaudible, giving the spectators time to review their private thoughts and still their racing pulses.

Then the minister replaced his headgear and smiled at the citizens of Philadelphia.

He half-turned to the pirates, as if he were addressing them. But Daniel could see that he was really speaking to the crowd.

"O wicked men," he began, "You know that the sins for which you are about to die are mighty and many. But you also know that there is a kind and compassionate God who will forgive your dark deeds, even at this late moment.

"If you will make an honest repentance before this assembly, you will be favorably received at the throne of judgment and will not bear the full brunt of the Creator's fury. Otherwise, the eternal fires of the underworld await you.

"In the final weeks before this execution, I have visited you men daily, sharing the dankness of your cell and endeavoring to impart the wisdom of the Scriptures. I take heart in knowing that my words did not fall on deaf ears. I have seen that the glory of God's word has ignited the fires of shame in your minds and that you are now ready to face the terrible magnitude of your crimes. I see that you are prepared to receive the full measure of God's mercy."

The minister gave the crowd a thin smile.

"The pirates have asked that they each have a few moments to atone for their sins. We will begin with Mr. Morgan."

He turned and nodded to Hatchet Jack. The small man was silent.

The minister leaned close to his ear and whispered something.

The pirate lifted his head, gazing at the sky.

"I am not afraid of death," Hatchet Jack said, his voice rising high and shrill above the crowd. "And I am not afraid of the gallows. But I am afraid of the great God and of the judgment that is to come. I have little to say, except that I have lived a vile and wicked life.

"If there are any amongst you who might be tempted to follow my sorry example, I say unto you: Avoid the sea rover's life. Avoid boisterous company and strong drink. But most of all, avoid the seductions of wealth and glory, for they are hollow rewards.

"I am deeply vexed that my own mother might someday learn of my dark deeds and might think that she had somehow failed to teach her son . . ."

Here the pirate hung his head and wept silently for several moments, his shoulders heaving, his breath coming in fast, shallow gasps.

It was a heartbreaking moment. All across the crowd, handkerchiefs appeared, like fluttering moths.

When Hatchet Jack recovered his composure, his eyes were luminous with tears.

"I repent for all that I have done," he continued, "and forgive those who are about to take my life, for I know they do it justly, as instruments of the great and powerful God. May He have mercy on my scandalous and wretched soul."

Daniel saw heads nodding approvingly and people whispering to their neighbors.

Then Daniel saw the minister nod to the hangman. He saw the swift arc of the executioner's knife, the taut cord that parted like a strand of hair, the thin form of Hatchet Jack dropping through the floor.

Most cruel of all, Daniel saw the pirate's body leap against the rope and spin like a top, making a weird shadow on the ground. For a few horrible moments, Jack violently scissored his legs in the air. With a merciful suddenness, the thrashing body went limp, swaying like a clock pendulum, his filthy bare feet dangling just above the level of the street.

There was an eerie silence, broken only by the whispering

of the wind and the creaking of the gallows timbers.

Then the crowd erupted in a roar that shook the very air around Daniel's perch. Off in the distance, someone was beating on a drum.

Through all the noise and confusion, Skellington simply stood with the noose tight around his neck, surveying the boisterous crowd with a faint smile on his lips. He did not look down at the swaying body of his companion. He did not seem agitated or concerned. He seemed to Daniel as if he were smiling into the very face of Death.

The minister stepped forward and raised his hand. Again the sudden silence filled the commons.

"Now," the clergyman said, "another sinner will speak to you."

He nodded to Skellington.

A hush settled over the crowd. The vagrant wind came up again, blowing from the east, flapping the tail of the executioner's long coat.

Skellington squared his shoulders and began, speaking in a fine voice that carried far over the heads of the crowd.

"You have heard a repentance speech from Hatchet Jack," he said, "but I can assure you, you won't hear one from me."

There was a moment of stunned silence. Then a few drunkards by the wine cart began laughing.

The minister glanced long and hard at the pirate, his eyes burning like fire coals, as if he were willing him to silence.

Skellington smiled back.

"I think you should know," he said, "that what you have

just heard were not Jack's words. Oh, no—that touching confession was written for him by this soul-grabbing minister."

The crowd rumbled.

The clergyman, visibly shaking with anger, nodded to the hangman.

But before the knife could be set to the rope, Skellington shouted, "Can't a dying man speak? Can't his last words be heard?"

"Yes, let the man speak," Daniel heard a man under the tree say.

"Let him speak," people all around were saying.

It occurred to Daniel that the crowd was interested in entertainment, not justice, and did not wish to end this bizarre spectacle until it had wrung the last drop of drama from the pirate's death.

The minister glanced nervously at the crowd. He motioned for the man in black to put his knife away.

Again the crowd cheered.

When it was quiet again, Skellington spoke, his voice ringing off the brick walls of the buildings that bounded the commons.

"For seven years, " the pirate said, "I have lived the life of a pirate. And I regret not a day of it.

"My friends, I have seen sights no landbound soul can even dream of.

"I have fought and adventured beside the bravest and most hearty companions a man could ever wish to know.

"I have tasted strong drink and howled at the ocean moon.

"And now that the Man with the Silver Oar has come for me at last, I go without repentance or complaint."

He gestured to the minister.

"This official calls men like us pirates, we who rob but little and sail under the flag of our own courage. But he and those like him—they are the real pirates. They are the ones who drain the lifeblood from you each day, with their tariffs and taxes and laws. They are the ones who keep your children in bondage and your elders in debtor's prison."

"He's right about that!" a man beside the wine cart shouted.

"Right as rain!" an old woman blurted out.

"And so," Skellington continued, "to any young men who might be tempted to follow my example, I would say: Be bold, be bold!

"Take to the sea!

"Take up the pistol and the sword and claim what is rightfully yours!"

The crowd cheered. Many young men were on their feet, shouting.

The minister had reached the limit of his patience. He nodded to the man in black.

"Break free!" the pirate shouted, his voice disappearing under a tidal wave of cheers.

Daniel watched as the executioner drew his knife and, with a swift, practiced motion, sliced through the cord. The trapdoor dropped.

Daniel closed his eyes.

But the crowd raised such a howl that he couldn't help

but open them and look.

And there was Skellington, going hand-over-hand up the gallows rope. He had snapped the cord that bound his wrists and was climbing like a wild animal above the heads of his executioners. As Daniel watched in amazement, the pirate swung one leg up and straddled the wooden beam. Looking down at the crowd, he tore the noose from around his neck and flung it away.

The hangman reached up and caught Skellington by the ankle. He raised his blade and was about to sink it into the pirate's calf when Skellington lashed out with his free foot, kicking the big man in the face. The hangman took two stumbling steps backward and toppled off the edge of the platform, falling like a slaughtered ox into the crowd.

Skellington dropped barefoot to the platform. From there, it was just a small leap to the executioner's wagon seat. He snatched up the long leather reins, pulling them free from the post, and lashed the horses across their hindquarters. The black stallions reared and plunged forward, into the heart of the crowd. People tumbled against one another in their haste to leap away. Some did not make it and were trampled as the mounts surged forward.

The soldiers began shooting, aiming high and wild. A musket ball tore through the air and slammed into the tree trunk above Daniel's head.

"May the Virgin save us!" Tuck swore, clinging to the tree.

Now the people beneath them were running toward the shelter of the buildings, shouting and trampling one another in their terror. The muskets were still going off, covering the commons with a haze of bluish gun smoke. The shots cut through the leaves overhead, slicing them from the branches.

Cautiously Daniel peered from the side of the tree. He and Tuck were in a very dangerous position, exposed to the gunfire. But that was not the worst of it. Daniel could see that Skellington was headed their way, the wagon cutting a broad swath through the terrified crowd.

There was one final problem: Skellington didn't see the tree until too late. Suddenly, there it was, blocking his path. At the last moment, Daniel saw him strain at the reins, pulling the horses off to the right. One of the stallions stumbled and fell, dragging the other down with him.

Daniel watched as the front wheels shattered. The wagon pitched forward and tumbled end-for-end, striking the tree with such force that the boys had to hold tight to keep from being knocked to the ground.

The air was thick with dust. Below them, the horses screamed and flailed with their hooves. They tore loose from the wagon and rolled to their feet, rearing wild-eyed before the crowd. They pranced and snorted, looking for an opening in the wall of bodies. A knot of terrified spectators pulled back, allowing the stallions to escape and head for open ground along the riverbank.

The wagon lay on its side, one wheel spinning rapidly.

A wedge of soldiers shouted and elbowed their way through the mob, reaching the base of the tree. For several tense moments, they searched through the wreckage, looking for a body. But there was no sign of Skellington.

The naval officer was there, in the midst of the confusion. He had drawn his sword and stood in the center of the swirling crowd, his mouth a grim, determined line.

He was the only one not shouting. He was the only one who looked up, peering into the foliage where the boys clung to the trunk. He narrowed his eyes, looking straight into Daniel's face. Too late, the boy ducked behind the trunk. He knew he had been seen.

But the officer was not looking for a boy. Gripping his sword, he turned and plunged back into the crowd.

The soldiers searched the area for several minutes more, fanning out across the commons. But the pirate was gone, vanished like a midsummer's breeze.

Then, when he thought the excitement was over, Daniel saw something. Over by the river, in the shadow of the waterfront pier, a well-built man with long, dark hair slipped from the edge of the crowd and sank into the muddy shallows of the Delaware.

Daniel could see the telltale ripples on the surface of the river—the sleek form was swimming away.

Then, for just an instant, he saw him once more: The swimmer surfaced, took a breath, then dove deep, headed downstream, toward the sea.

CHAPTER TWO

❧

*F*OR A SOLID HOUR after the pirate's escape, the good citizens of Philadelphia wandered around the execution dock, giddy with excitement. Every tongue was moving, every hand was gesturing wildly.

Daniel and Tuck were trapped in the tree until the crowd thinned out. They watched as the apprentices cut Hatchet Jack's body down and laid him out on the street, setting to work with the tar brushes.

Meanwhile the men at the wine cart and the children with the handbills did a brisk business. Up in the side streets, the tavern doors were opened wide, welcoming anyone with a dry throat and coins in his purse.

By the time Tuck and Daniel touched solid ground, the commons were emptying out. The riverine tide rose and covered the footings of the gallows timbers.

Tuck patted his pockets as if he were missing something. He swore quietly.

"Did you bring your jackknife?" he asked. "Looks like I left mine in the toolbox."

Daniel fumbled in his pocket and handed over his blade.

"Come along," Tuck said, taking the knife. "I'll show you

how we take a trophy. Powerful magic in a hangman's rope, especially one that still has the scent of death on it. I can sell it to the gypsy woman who brings the apple cart 'round to the yard."

Then Tuck stopped and looked into Daniel's eyes for the first time, seeing the haunted look that had settled there.

He clapped him on the shoulder.

"I understand how you feel," he said. "It does seize a person up, don't it, seeing someone kilt like that, right before your eyes?"

Daniel could only nod and follow dumbly as Tuck walked across the commons to the gallows.

The deadly timbers were deserted now, creaking in the wind. Jack's rope still hung from the main beam. Tuck had to wade out into the muddy water and reach up high over his head to cut himself a length of it. After a few moments of steady sawing, the thick rope came away in his hand. He tucked it into his belt and waded up onto the bank. He knew better than to offer Daniel a piece of his souvenir. Tuck closed the clasp knife and handed it back to its owner.

"See you in the morning," Tuck said. "You'll be there, won't you?"

"I will be there," Daniel said.

Tuck nodded and slipped away, leaving Daniel alone by the gallows.

It was too late to go back to the shipyard and too early to go home. If Daniel wanted to, he could be at his uncle's house in a matter of moments. But he was not ready for that, not just now. So he simply wandered, letting his feet guide him through the town. The streets were crowded, and that was good. No one would notice an aimless boy among so many noisy people.

Tuck was right about the hanging, Daniel thought. It did seize a person up to see a man lose his life in such a public, gruesome manner. But Hatchet Jack's death, as horrible as it was, was not the thing that had turned Daniel inside out. No, it was the defiant speech of the pirate, Moses Skellington.

For the first time in his life, he had heard the words of a man who was not afraid to challenge the awesome authority of the crown. Here was a man who did exactly as he pleased, without asking the permission of magistrates or ministers or even King George himself.

What were Skellington's words?

"Be bold, be bold! Take to the sea! Claim what is rightfully yours!"

At that moment, Daniel thought his life seemed very fragile, ready to crumble into dust. The thirst for this outrageous kind of freedom was like a powerful drink. And the fact that it was beyond his reach made it all the more tantalizing.

Daniel's mind sped ahead of his body, into a hurricane of dangerous thoughts: He tried to imagine himself slipping into the river as Skellington had and floating away downstream, leaving behind the dreary world of sawdust pits and Sunday dinners, following the watery track to some secret meeting place along the riverbanks.

By now, Daniel imagined Skellington was far away, joining his shipmates at some river cave or swampside tavern. Daniel could see the hearty buccaneers gathering by a bonfire as darkness fell, celebrating Skellington's brave escape from the gallows, drinking a farewell toast to Hatchet Jack, and planning their next adventure.

He could picture it clearly: The dancing firelight, a round drinking table heaped with scrolls of exotic maps, the names of distant lands rolling off the sailor's lips like strange poetry: Malibar and Tahiti and the Far Tortugas. The talk of plunder and riches would be intoxicating.

Daniel saw himself barefoot and free, in the summer night, free from the strictures of Quaker society and the senseless rules of city life.

Suddenly Daniel felt a hand on his shoulder.

"Excuse me, but you're the Collins boy, aren't you?"

Daniel swallowed. It was the naval officer with the splendid sword. Suddenly, Daniel was back on the cobblestone streets of the Philadelphia, in the stench of the milling crowd.

"Daniel Collins, isn't it?" the officer said.

Daniel could not get any voice up out of his throat, so he simply nodded.

The officer smiled. "Yes, of course you are. I thought I recognized you at the hanging—you were one of the young fellows up in the tree."

Daniel's face grew hot. To be discovered this way, after being so obedient for so long! What if his uncle should find out?

"I don't expect you'll remember me," the officer continued, "but I knew your aunt and uncle years ago. I am from
New York, but my mother and your aunt Terra were friends
when they were girls, right here in Philadelphia. Do you
mind if I walk with you? I have been invited to have dinner
with your uncle tonight, and I am not sure I know the way."

"Dinner?" Daniel said.

"Yes, along with the shipyard owner, Thomas Greyling. I
have not been in Philadelphia in several years, and Mister
Greyling and I have some business matters to discuss with
your uncle . . ."

Daniel turned to face the man.

"Listen, sir, speaking of my uncle—"

"Please, call me James," he said, "Lieutenant James
Mainwaring, at your service."

Daniel took a deep breath. "My uncle must not know
that I was at the execution today. You see, it is not permitted . . ."

Mainwaring smiled.

"Say no more," he said lightly. "The secret of your indis-
cretion is safe with me. And let me give you a piece of
advice."

He leaned forward and whispered: "Don't look so guilty.
You are not the first Quaker boy to sneak off to a hanging."

"Really?" Daniel asked. He was flooded with relief.

"I assure you, it happens all the time," Mainwaring said.

Daniel sighed, relaxing a little.

"Everyone has secrets," Mainwaring said. "Yours is safe
with me. Now let's get to dinner. I have lived on hardtack

and brined beef for the last month. A decent meal will set well about now."

Daniel nodded and turned toward home.

They were leaving the commercial district, walking into the Quaker area, where the three-story brick buildings rose fine and straight from the tree-lined streets. They walked past impressive churches and somber graveyards.

Daniel knew he was fortunate to live here, in the jewel of the British Colonies. He knew that the fair town of Philadelphia was the dream of the great Quaker visionary, William Penn.

He had heard the story many times: Forty years before, Penn had been given a huge tract of land in the North American wilderness by England's King Charles II to repay a debt owed to Penn's father, a trusted advisor and commander of Britain's naval forces.

But William Penn was no military man. He was a dreamer who was attracted to the teachings of an English Quaker named George Fox. Fox urged people to break with the Anglican Church of England and follow a simpler religion. He declared that God spoke to each person, without the needless interference of ministers and church officials.

Penn dreamed of creating a prosperous society in the New World, where tolerance and truth would be the guiding lights. When the king offered him land in America, the young man picked a beautiful spot along the Delaware River and began to make his dream a reality. He was astonishingly successful.

Penn's "greene countrie towne" was soon surrounded by

bountiful farms, pleasantly situated along the river. The Delaware River faithfully carried the farmers' produce to the markets of the world. The major crop was wheat, and the principal customers were the slave-holding sugar plantations in the Caribbean Islands.

These islands, colonized by Spain and France, and later dominated by England, had become incredibly profitable. Sugar was king, and the steady flow of slave labor to the large sugar plantations was an essential ingredient to the plan's success.

The shining city around them was evidence of the brilliance of Penn's vision.

As they neared his block on Spruce Street, Daniel was struck, as always, by how this section of the city seemed so far removed from the dirt and squalor of the waterfront. Although separated by a short distance, the two areas were a world apart.

Mainwaring glanced at Daniel's filthy work clothes.

"Have you become a chimney sweep?" he asked.

"No. I am a carpenter's apprentice at the shipyard. For a while, I served as a clerk for Mr. Greyling in his office. That was a clean job, but I have no head for figures and my handwriting is very poor. So I was sent to the sawpit with the common boys."

"Shipbuilding is a fine profession."

"I would rather be sailing them," Daniel said.

"Well, perhaps in a few years, you will."

Daniel shook his head.

"I do not think so," he said. "I am afraid the best I will

ever become is a shipyard carpenter. Uncle has forbidden me even to set foot on a sailing ship."

"Why is that?"

"You may remember that my father was lost at sea."

Mainwaring nodded sadly. "Yes, of course. Do you remember anything of your father?" he asked.

"A little. I was only six when he died. And he wasn't home much. But I do remember that he would take me down to the river and we would roll our trousers to our knees and wade in the shallows. I still see him that way, sometimes."

Mainwaring nodded.

"And your mother? How did she weather your father's death?"

"She died of the fever a year later."

"Ah, yes. And so you are an orphan."

Daniel shook his head.

"Not really. You see, I come from a long line of ocean-going men. We have always stood together: 'Blood is thicker than water' is our family motto. My grandfather was the original owner of our ship, the *Good Samaritan*, back in England. When he died, the ship passed to his only sons.

"That's when my father and Uncle Elias decided to come to the Colonies and establish a shipping business here in Philadelphia. My older sister Hettie and I, along with our parents, lived here on Spruce Street with Aunt Terra and Uncle Elias, who never had children. Our family had taken on the Quaker faith by then. After the death of our parents, my sister and I remained with our uncle and aunt."

Mainwaring frowned.

"I know a little of how you must feel," he said quietly. "My own father was a navy man, killed in a battle with the French off the coast of England. Nasty business. My mother did not die, but she might as well have. She became like a ghost, wandering the house with her Bible and her tears.

"Still, I yearned to go to sea—like my father. But Mother would not hear of it. She tried to send me to scribner's school. I knew that would be the end of me. Eventually, I just had to take matters into my own hands."

"What did you do?" Daniel asked.

Mainwaring smiled thinly, "I shipped myself to sea in a wooden box."

"What? How did that work?"

"Not very well," Mainwaring said, laughing. "It was a crazy thing to do. I built a box, just big enough for me to sit up in. I drilled airholes in the sides. I convinced a few well-meaning friends among the dockworkers to take part in my brilliant scheme. They smuggled me aboard a British gun-ship and lashed my container down in the hold. Unfortunately, in all the confusion, they set the box in upside down.

"I spent the next twelve hours in the most awkward posi-tion. I tried to turn, but the box was too narrow. At last, I couldn't stand it anymore, and I hollered until I was blue in the face. One of the seamen came down and pried me out. They set me to swabbing the deck that very afternoon.

"That was the beginning of my life at sea. But they soon learned who I was. The captain had shipped with my father when they were young men and he took pity on me. Before

I knew it, I was a gunner's assistant on a British man-o-war. A few small shrapnel wounds, a few moments of conspicuous bravery, a few favors in the right places, and I was commissioned an officer.

"My first assignment was to take a small sloop and root out smugglers along the Jersey coast. Turned out I was pretty good at it. One thing led to another, and when the King began offering rewards for captured pirates, I saw my chance. I volunteered for special duty, and I have been a pirate hunter for two years now. Officially I am on a leave of absence from the navy, hiring myself and my crew out to anyone who will supply us with a ship and send us to sea."

"But why are you in the city today?" Daniel asked.

"I was the one who captured Skellington and Morgan off the coast of Jersey. I was hoping to see them both hanged today."

"What an escape!" Daniel said admirably. Then, as soon as the words were out of his mouth, he regretted them.

Mainwaring smiled sadly. "Yes, Skellington got away, sure enough. We were hoping to make an example of him. But he is a small fish. I cannot trouble my thoughts with him any longer. I have other matters to consider, matters I must discuss with your uncle."

"By the way," the officer said, "I am a little uneasy about meeting him after all these years. I was just a youth when I saw him last. I know he does not approve of the military. So if I do anything un-Quakerly, give me a kick under the table, will you?"

Daniel nodded.

Captain Collins' dwelling on Spruce Street was coming into view now, a modest house of red brick with a fine slate roof. Two magnificent cherry trees arched over the front door, heavy with glistening fruit.

At that moment, the front door was flung open and Hettie came out in a flowing dress, her face as radiant as a new moon.

"James," she said, "thee hast come back to us!"

Mainwaring stopped in his tracks. His eyes widened.

And Daniel knew that Hettie, with a single glance, had captured another admirer.

"Hedabelle," Mainwaring said, "you are no longer a child . . ."

Hettie laughed, looking up at him with shining eyes.

"I am eighteen," she said cheerfully. "And, thee, James. Thee hast become such a handsome, gallant . . ."

"Yes," Mainwaring said quietly, "we are all grown up now."

Daniel shifted uneasily. They were both ignoring him. He slipped away, going down the alleyway to the side gate and into the garden.

He knew Aunt Terra would have a pail for washing and a set of clean clothes hanging by the grape arbor. This was their daily routine. She would not permit him to enter the house until he was washed and changed, free of shipyard grime.

Of course, Daniel was never entirely free of grime. No matter how hard he scrubbed with Aunt Terra's harsh yellow soap, he could not get the dirt from the crevices around his knuckles. His hair, he knew, looked as if it had been combed with a tar brush. And his stiff dinner clothes, his dark jacket and trousers, and his white shirt, never seemed to fit him properly. His highly polished boots were stiff as wood.

Daniel hated the formal dinners at his uncle's house. Because Uncle Elias was a respected businessman who owned and sailed his own ship, he often entertained important merchants and government officials when he was home from his voyages. Daniel dreaded the long hours of conversation, feeling imprisoned and yet invisible in his chair.

As for Aunt Terra, she was a thick-necked, red-faced woman who had made it her full-time occupation to host dinner parties for her husband and to orchestrate the comings and goings of Hettie's young admirers, searching for the best match—always searching, but never satisfied. She knew Hettie was a rare jewel, their only female relative, and not to be given away lightly.

But tonight might be different, Daniel thought, as he pulled his work shirt over his head. Lieutenant Mainwaring would certainly add some spark to the dinner conversation.

It was then Daniel noticed the bullet hole in the side of his shirt. It was about the size of a grape, two holes actually, one going in, one coming out. He poked his forefinger through them in amazement. Then he understood: As he had clung to an overhead branch, the stray bullet had passed through the loose cloth bunched around his waist and had exited just below his right armpit, missing his heart by inches.

Daniel's pulse began to race. Suddenly every particle in

his body was awake and alive. He had been shot at—and missed. Without knowing exactly why, he felt intensely satisfied.

So, he thought, this is what it feels like to have a real adventure.

He knew he had broken one of his uncle's ironclad rules. But he also knew that, on some deep and unexplainable level, it had been worth it.

Dropping his dirty shirt, he went to the washstand where the tools of cleanliness were laid out like a surgeon's instruments. As he dipped his hands into the pail, he smiled.

Maybe the dinner tonight would not be so boring.

CHAPTER THREE

～◦～

$\mathcal{A}$s Daniel entered the house, he heard the murmur of voices coming from the dining room. Silently he crept past the kitchen, where the indentured servant, a lowland English girl named Sarah Stewart, was already ladling the onion soup into a half-dozen bowls set on a hand-crafted tray.

When Daniel walked into the wood-paneled room, he could see that everyone else was already seated. Even though the summer sky remained light, the tiny windows and thick walls made the dining room seem like a dark cavern, lit only by a few flickering candles.

At the head of the table sat his uncle, Elias Collins (or Captain Collins, as he preferred to be called). Even when he was on land, the captain moved with the authority of a man who expected to be obeyed. He was dressed in simple but dignified clothing, a dark waistcoat with a white cravat at his throat.

Collins was tall and angular, with a great hawklike nose and deep-set, serious eyes. From the time Daniel was a small child, he had suspected that his uncle could peer into his soul with those piercing eyes, seeing anything hidden there. So he hid very little.

When the captain saw his nephew hesitating in the doorway, he nodded to the empty seat beside him.

"Here thou art," Collins said gravely.

"Good to see thee, Uncle," Daniel said. He nodded to the others and took his place.

Daniel knew how to stay in his place. In the captain's world, there was a place for everything and everyone. And woe unto the man, woman, or child who stepped out of place.

Here in the household, for instance, Quaker manners were always observed. The use of the biblical words "thee" and "thine" were sprinkled through everyday speech. This was the Society of Friends' "Holy Conversation," a way of speaking that was not proud or boastful, but full of quiet compassion and an enduring appreciation for the value of simple things.

Daniel glanced around the oval table. To the captain's left was Aunt Terra, radiant with laughter. Beside her, in a glow of warm candlelight, sat Hettie: dark hair, dark eyes, skin like fine china, high cheekbones that shone in the muted light. To Daniel's right, directly across the table from his sister, sat Lieutenant Mainwaring, who gave him a jaunty wink when he slid into his place.

At the far end of the table sat Thomas Greyling, the tall, iron-haired shipmaster who was active in the Anglican Church and often worked with Captain Collins on charitable causes. Although the city was dominated by the Quakers, the Church of England was still a powerful influence, and men like Greyling acted as skillful middlemen in the gritty machinery of colonial politics.

Greyling nodded solemnly in Daniel's direction. But the boy knew he had been a disappointment to the two older men, and that knowledge made him meek in their presence.

"Now that we are all assembled," Captain Collins said, "I will ask for a moment of silent reflection. Shall we clasp hands?"

All around, heads were bowed. To his left, Daniel felt his uncle's hand, gripping his. On his right, Mainwaring's strong, lean hand closed around his own. They closed their eyes and sat in quiet meditation and thanksgiving. The only sound was the creaking of the floorboards as the servant girl moved in the kitchen.

"And now," Captain Collins said, lifting his head and smiling, "let us enjoy this wonderful feast Mrs. Collins has planned for us."

Aunt Terra turned her head toward the kitchen.

"Sarah," she called, "we are ready, dear."

Sarah Stewart was at the captain's elbow, setting a steaming bowl before him. The delicious aroma of peppery onion soup filled the room.

Mainwaring laid aside his napkin and stood, raising his glass. Sarah had poured each of them a generous ration of brandy.

"Captain . . . Mrs. Collins . . . with your kind permission, I would like to offer a toast," he said.

The captain nodded gravely.

"Go right ahead," Aunt Terra said.

34

Mainwaring cleared his throat.

"It is so good," Mainwaring said, "to be back in the loving circle of my old friends once again. I have been away too long and hope that I can renew our intimacy in the weeks to come."

His eyes did not stray from Hettie's as he lifted the glass to his mouth. She drank as well, touching the rim of the glass to her lips. A smile played at the corners of her mouth.

None of this was lost on Terra, who peered at Mainwaring through heavily lidded eyes, appraising, calculating.

Daniel lifted his glass, taking a small sip. It went down smartly, making his teeth tingle. Good brandy.

When Mainwaring had seated himself, Captain Collins lifted his spoon. The others did not need to be invited. They supped for several moments in refined satisfaction.

"Friend James," Captain Collins said at last, dabbing his mouth with a blue linen napkin, "we have heard that thou hast chosen a life at sea."

The officer nodded. "Yes, Captain, I have."

"And does thee find it a satisfactory life?"

The young man smiled.

"More than satisfactory," he said. And then, raising an eyebrow at Hettie, he added, "Although not without its dangers."

"I am sure you are in danger on a daily basis," Hettie murmured softly.

"Nonsense," Captain Collins said. "The sea is only dangerous to fools and sinners. Prudent men may sail before the wind, sound in God's protection."

"My dear Captain," Thomas Greyling chuckled, "you are too modest. Not all men have your skill—or your luck. The crew of the *Good Samaritan* is fortunate to have such a knowledgeable captain at her helm. Many a poor sailor has met disaster on the high seas. Many have succumbed to dangers of storms or the ravages of illness or, worst of all, to the savagery of pirates."

Collins frowned.

"This is not a subject for a Quaker table," he stated. "Storms and fever are real enough. But the danger of pirates is greatly exaggerated," he said.

Greyling laid down his spoon.

"Captain Collins, are you aware that today a pirate was hanged in our own city?" he asked.

"Unfortunately I am," the Captain said.

"And you do not approve?" Greyling said tightly.

"Friend Thomas," Collins said sternly, "thou knows I do not."

"But why?"

"We have already had this discussion. Thou knows that violence begets violence."

"That is no answer," Greyling said testily. "If the Quaker majority does not put aside this pretense of pacifism and enter into the hard work of policing these ruffians—"

"Forgive me, Mr. Greyling," Mainwaring said, "but may I intervene? I have some firsthand knowledge of the subject. With your permission, Captain?"

Collins nodded, leaning back in his chair.

Daniel was about to kick Mainwaring under the table,

then changed his mind. He wanted to hear what the young officer had to say.

All eyes were on the handsome lieutenant.

"My friends," Mainwaring began, "from Boston to Barbados, the waters are infested with pirates. At the present time, there are perhaps two thousand men who have joined the pirate cause. If we assume fifty men to a ship, this means that there are more than forty pirate ships hounding our coastline.

"The Royal Navy, I am sorry to say, has been preoccupied with matters in other parts of the empire. The Lord High Admiral has only given us four warships to patrol the entire eastern coastline and another four to protect the watery maze of the Caribbean.

"This is laughably insufficient. As you know, the eastern seaboard is a network of river estuaries, bays, inlets, and islands. There are a thousand places to hide, a thousand sheltered coves where pirate sloops can lay in waiting, ready to capture any merchant ship that comes their way.

"But things are changing. The colonies now have the right to try and hang pirates, instead of taking them all the way to London. Last year, King George issued a proclamation declaring that any pirate who will lay down his arms and surrender his ship will be given a full pardon.

"The King has also offered a reward for anyone who captures a pirate chieftain and his crew. Bounty hunters, usually off-duty naval officers, who handpick their own crews and raise private funds to outfit their own ships, are seeking the reward.

"And this, Captain, is why Mister Greyling and I have come to you tonight: To ask your help in bringing these sea dogs to justice. With help from you and your Quaker brethren—"

"I do not agree with thy methods," Captain Collins said tersely.

Mainwaring continued, undaunted.

"Fine," he said. "But let me ask you this: Have you ever been pursued by pirates?"

The captain stared back at him, unruffled.

"On occasion," he admitted.

"And have you and your crew fought them off?"

"Decidedly not," the Quaker said. "I would not bloody my hand against another man. I have found that a swift vessel is the best defense. On every occasion, I have been able to outrun the scoundrels, without a shot fired or a man harmed."

Terra broke in, saying, "Such talk around our peaceful table! If we must talk of bravery, I might mention the time the good captain sailed into the very teeth of a hurricane on the Carolina coast, taking food and medicine to the stranded inhabitants of the lowland ports. Or perhaps it would not be out of place to mention his role in quelling the yellow fever epidemic which struck the Caribbean islands just last year."

"Please, Terra," Captain Collins said soothingly, "I am sure that these minor exploits would not be of interest to these gentlemen."

Aunt Terra closed her mouth, casting her eyes down.

"I can assure you, Mrs. Collins," Mainwaring said boldly, "robbery at sea is a matter of life and death. The entire shipping business is suffering tremendous losses, even as we speak! Some merchant vessels are even beginning to carry gunnery crews and cannons as a precautionary measure."

"It is foolishness," Captain Collins said. "The freebooters will only capture these weapons and add them to their stores.

"Do not attempt to outfight these ruffians. Outsail them instead. I have discovered that pirates, as a group, are not very good seamen. It doesn't take much to outmaneuver them. A ragtag drunken crew, sailing a ship they have just stolen the week before, is no match for the men of the *Good Samaritan*."

"I have been aboard many a pirate vessel, and I have looked into the faces of many of these scoundrels," Mainwaring added, "and I will confirm what you say. As individuals, most of them are murderous cowards. They are only troublesome when they travel in packs. After all, how much courage does it really take to do what they do?

"The average merchant ship, because of lack of space and a wish to economize, is manned by a small crew, usually less than a dozen men. They carry very little in the way of weapons or armaments.

"A pirate ship will carry six or ten cannons bolted to her deck and as many men as can swarm aboard, perhaps fifty or sixty. They are armed to the teeth and have no compunctions about slitting the throat of anyone who stands in their way.

"With this unfair advantage, how much courage does it really take for them to run down and capture a merchant vessel? If they can get within hailing distance, they can take her by sheer force.

"And they do not fight squarely. They have many treacherous wiles for drawing close to our ships. They carry a trunkful of flags and can change their nationality and appearance at will. They often disguise their own ships as merchant vessels. Sometimes the men even dress in women's clothing and attempt to lure innocent ships to them by pretending that the crew is down with sickness and that they must be rescued."

"There are pirates everywhere, Uncle," Hettie put in. "Why, that dreadful pirate was hung just a few blocks from where we sit. A man named John Ax or some such. And one of the wretched criminals even escaped."

"Just last week," she continued, "I heard that the pirate Jack Scarfield looted and burned a heavily laden merchant, I believe it was the *Baltimore Belle*, right off the point of Cape May, within sight of land."

"It is true," Greyling said. " I spoke to a gentleman who saw it with his own eyes. This is an outrage!"

"There is no question in my mind," Mainwaring declared, "that Scarfield is the most dangerous man in the colonies. Tell me, Captain Collins, have you ever encountered the notorious Captain Scarfield? I am told that he has command of an unmistakable ship, a swift craft called the *Revenge* which openly flies the Jolly Roger. It is studded with cannons and has bloodred sails."

Elias Collins smiled and laid down his spoon. "I have not met with him myself, and I have not seen such a ship. But I can tell thee this: He is a very overrated criminal. If Scarfield had truly sunk all of the ships credited to him, there would be no room on the bottom of the ocean for fish.

"There is nothing remarkable about this man, except that he has captured the imagination of the populace. Tongues have wagged, making him a bit of a legend. This man is nothing more than a fashionable rumor."

"But tell me this, sir," Mainwaring asked. "If you were being boarded by a pirate like Scarfield, would you not kill him to preserve your own life?"

"Thou knows I would not."

"But why?"

"Because then I would be a murderer. And in killing him, I would kill the light of life in myself. If a man survives by murdering his fellows, his mortal flesh may remain intact. But someday, be he pirate or honest man, he must die. And, whether he ends his life peacefully in his own bed or at the point of a sword, it is the cleanliness of the spirit that will prevail."

Hettie, seeking to head off a theological debate, said, "But Uncle, if men like James could sweep the waters clean of pirates, that would be a good thing, wouldn't it?"

Captain Collins raised his glass.

"That would be a very good thing, Hettie. But before we accomplish that, I would rather make the streets of Philadelphia safe for our wives and children. I must say, I feel more danger on our city streets at night than I ever have

41

in the midst of a pirate attack. I have often said to my crew that a man should go to sea for safety, if nothing else."

Over that small joke, they turned to the sumptuous dinner before them, a platter of fresh-caught trout, smothered in wine sauce. Outside, darkness fell softly on the Quaker city.

After the meal, the women quietly retreated and Daniel was about to leave as well.

"Please, Daniel," Captain Collins said, "wilt thee stay with us awhile longer? It is time thee began to join in the conversations of men."

Daniel nodded, surprised to be included.

"Gentlemen," the captain said, taking one of the dining candles, "let us adjourn to the library."

Daniel was suddenly aware of how tall his uncle was beside other men: He towered over both Mainwaring and Greyling.

Daniel followed the delegation out of the dining room and down a short hallway into Captain Collins' study, a snug room whose walls were lined with shelves of ancient books. Beside the unlit fireplace, comfortable chairs were arranged in a small half-circle.

When the men were seated, Captain Collins drew out his tobacco pouch and began filling a long-stemmed clay pipe. Taking a broom straw and touching it to the nearby candle flame, he lit the bowl and puffed silently for several moments, his eyes dark and somber in the leaping flame.

With this permission to smoke, Mainwaring drew a slender West Indies cigar from his tunic and leaned into the candle flame, puffing until the end glowed orange in the half-darkness.

Greyling sat with his hands laced around one knee, staring at the floorboards.

"Friend Thomas," the captain said at last, "thee looks troubled."

Thomas Greyling sighed.

"Captain, I have the greatest admiration for your Quaker ideals. You are one of a handful of men who have managed to conduct a successful shipping business without sacrificing a shred of your moral rectitude. But in this case, your pacifist approach is simply not practical.

"The pirates are a very real disruption to our trade. Many of our city's merchants are desperate. We have appealed to the King for help, but what he has offered has been woefully insufficient."

Captain Collins took the pipe stem from his mouth.

"What do thee propose?"

Greyling nodded to Mainwaring.

The lieutenant leaned forward.

"Captain Collins," the young officer said earnestly, "as I mentioned before, in some of the coastal towns, the prominent merchants have engaged naval officers to run down the pirates. These bounty hunters do not get a single coin unless they capture a pirate ship and its crew. No prey, no pay."

Collins frowned. "And this, Lieutenant, is what thee would do?"

"Yes."

"Why hast thee come to me? Thee could certainly raise the funds through Mister Greyling's friends."

"We have come to you," Greyling said, "because we want Quaker support for this venture. As you are a merchant captain and a man of the sea yourself, I thought—"

"That I would bring the others along? Not a chance. Each man will vote his own conscience, regardless of what I say."

"But you have influence—"

"Influence has no sway when each man is voting his conscience, Thomas. I will not bloody my hand with this plan."

"Very well," Greyling said. "If I cannot appeal to you as a civic leader, perhaps I can speak to you as a businessman."

He leaned forward.

"The profits of this enterprise could be huge," he said in a half-whisper. "The captured goods will be divided among Lieutenant Mainwaring, his crew, and, most importantly, the investors."

Collins shook his head.

"Thomas," he said, "does thee truly think I would be tempted by this offer? I am surprised that thee hast stained thy good name with this dark adventure—"

"Good night," Greyling said abruptly, standing up. "When the conversation degenerates into a moral lecture, I know the evening is lost."

"Good night," Captain Collins said contentedly, puffing on his pipe. Greyling left without another word.

Mainwaring snubbed out his cigar.

"I will see myself out after I have thanked the women," the lieutenant said.

"Friend James," the Captain said, "I hope that my frank discussion of this matter has not blunted thy affection for our family. Thy mother and Terra were great friends, and I would only wish that the bonds between us should not be injured by ideological differences."

Mainwaring bowed.

"Of course not, Captain. You may rely upon my friendship, no matter what."

With a nod to Daniel, he turned and disappeared through the doorway. The sound of his boots faded away down the hall. In the kitchen, Daniel could hear the women's voices, high and mirthful.

Daniel and his uncle sat in the close darkness, saying nothing.

Outside, a carriage rattled by on the cobblestone street.

It occurred to Daniel that his uncle was lost in his own thoughts, and had forgotten he was there.

But he had not.

"Daniel," he said at last, "does thee know why I wanted to include thee in our discussion?"

"No, Uncle."

"Because the day will come when thee must take thy place in the Meeting, and in society at large. I want thee to understand that not all men think as we do."

Daniel nodded. This was not news. He rubbed shoulders every day with men at the shipyard who did not hold Quaker beliefs. But he said nothing.

Captain Collins sighed.

"I am afraid I did not convince them of the futility of

their approach," the Quaker said.

"No, Uncle," Daniel murmured.

"Tell me, Daniel," Captain Collins asked, "do thee remember the teaching 'Blood is thicker than water'?"

"Yes."

"And pray, what does thee think it means?"

Daniel looked down at the floorboards.

"I suppose it means that thee should always be loyal to thy relatives, to thy family."

The Captain nodded.

"Yes, Daniel," he said, "that is precisely what it means. Remember: Outside of God, family is the most important thing there is. Loyalty to thy family comes first. Then loyalty to thy Quaker brethren. These men do not think as we do, Daniel. Give them a wide berth. Do not allow thyself to become contaminated by their ways. This is the road to destruction. If thee are wise and patient, thee may find thyself in a position to carry on the family business. This is an awesome responsibility—to care for our wealth and traditions. Thee are, after all, the only male left in the family. Eventually, all that now belongs to me could be thine. I trust that someday thee will be equal to this."

Daniel swallowed. He had never seen the captain look at him so seriously.

"Yes, Uncle," was all he could manage. He had a sudden impulse to speak up, to forge ahead and broach the idea that he might someday be allowed to go to sea. But he realized he could no more do that than he could sprout wings and fly out the window.

"Is there something on thy mind?" Collins asked.

"No, Uncle," Daniel said quietly.

"Very well. Thee may go to thy rest now. I will sit up awhile yet."

"Good night, Uncle."

Captain Collins turned in the darkness, the pipe bowl glowing.

"Good night, Daniel," he said.

Daniel rose to his feet.

As he climbed the stairs to his attic room, his head was spinning with all he had heard that evening.

It was a warm night. Daniel swung the oval window wide open and let the breeze come into his musty room. Over the rooftops of the city, the moon was rising, yellow and full.

He caught a glimpse of movement in the garden below, over by the grape arbor. At first, he thought it might be a stray cat. Then he heard his sister's laughter. He caught sight of the two of them, seated in the dappled moonlight underneath the latticework of the arbor. And Daniel could see that Lieutenant Mainwaring was holding her hand to his heart.

CHAPTER FOUR

*I*N THE DAYS that followed, Mainwaring became a frequent visitor to the Collins household.

When Daniel came trudging home from work, he would often find Mainwaring and Captain Collins sitting in the shade under the sycamore, playing a game of chess, or drinking a glass of Jamaican rum. Collins seemed to take an interest in the young officer, and Daniel overheard many a good-natured theological debate, with neither changing the other's mind but each asserting the other's right to hold to his beliefs.

Daniel felt a pang of jealousy. He knew it was not a virtuous emotion, but he felt it all the same. He had been genuinely touched when his uncle had invited him to join the men after dinner. And he had been honored by the brief conversation afterward. For most of his life, Daniel had felt his uncle had ignored him. Now Mainwaring had come along. The officer was so much brighter, more entertaining, and more challenging.

One Sunday, Elias Collins even invited Mainwaring to put aside his sword and uniform and join them in worship at the Meeting House. But the officer politely declined, saying that he did not want to do anything that would embarrass them in front of their Quaker brethren.

On that particular day, the ordinarily peaceful gathering became something quite different. Just as they did every Sunday, the family had washed and dressed and set off for the four-block walk north on Front Street to the Meeting House by the Delaware River.

The Meeting House was a simple wood-frame building with high ceilings. The single spacious room was filled with rows of wooden benches. Men and women were seated separately, with men occupying one side of the room, ladies the other.

The service was simplicity itself: The place of worship was plain and undecorated. There was no choir and were no hymnbooks; no pulpit or minister.

Instead the congregation sat for a full hour in quiet contemplation. If anyone felt moved to speak, he or she would simply stand and address the assembly. There was no comment or debate, simply an honoring of The Word and an understanding that each person was, in his or her own way, a vessel of truth, capable of carrying messages from the Creator.

On this morning, Daniel occupied his usual place on the hard wooden bench beside the somber, silent form of his uncle. They were dressed in their usual dark woolen clothing, and Daniel could not ignore the trickle of sweat that ran between his shoulder blades, soaking into his clean white shirt. They had been sitting for a full quarter hour in silence when Daniel noticed his uncle getting to his feet.

"I had a dream last night," Elias Collins began.

Every ear was open, waiting.

At these times, Daniel was always struck by the change that came over his uncle. He was no longer the stern, taciturn sea captain. Instead he became the navigator of a deeper, more interior ocean. His voice, while strong and full, became dreamlike, almost tender. Sometimes he became choked with emotion, and several times he had wept openly with the beauty of The Word.

Daniel had seen many people tremble as they spoke at Meeting, which was one of the reasons the Society of Friends were known to outsiders as "Quakers."

"I had a dream," Captain Collins repeated, "and in my dream I saw the arrival of ships on our shores, carrying black people chained up to be sold like cattle in the marketplace. But, Friends, when I looked into their faces, I saw that these men and women were not strangers. No, they had the faces of myself and of every one of thee. I saw that this practice of slavery, which we allow to flourish here in our midst, is putting every one of us in chains.

"The enslavement of other men and women must end, my friends. And it must begin here, with us, in our own houses and fields."

Here the captain paused, drew a kerchief from his pocket, and wiped his face. Then he silently took his seat.

He had no sooner settled onto the bench than a voice from several rows back said, "But Friend Elias, surely thee will admit thee have a servant in thine own house."

Dozens of heads turned in the speaker's direction. It was

Thomas Small, a tinsmith. He was tall and thin and licked his lips nervously as he spoke.

"If a well-respected man such as thyself—" he continued. But he never got to finish.

Across the room, Terra Collins sprang to her feet.

"Friend Thomas," she declared hotly, "thee knows that Sarah Stewart is no slave. She is an indentured servant, sure enough. We paid her passage from England. And in seven years, she shall have her freedom, just as we do."

A white-bearded elder raised his hand.

"Please," he said. "The purpose here is not to accost thy neighbor."

For a moment, Terra and Thomas glared at each other. Then they each sat. But the air was humming with tension.

A burly man near the front of the hall stood with his hands on his hips.

"As thou knows, I am a wheat farmer. And I say without flinching that I am also a slaveholder. Many of thee have been to my farm south of the Landing. Many have seen the fields of wheat that ripen in the sun. But how many have thought about the labor that is required to wrest this crop from the soil?

"Captain Collins, hast thee ever taken a sickle and gone into the fields in the heat of summer? Hast thee shivered in the mud during spring planting? Hast thee considered the pure animal work that goes into reaping the crop that thy own ship carries to the West Indies? I have only two sons, Friend Elias. Without the work of the dark men, I would never be able to bring my wheat to the docks. Before thee speak, consider the impact thy words may have on thy own livelihood!"

An old woman shot to her feet.

"Friend Cutler! I reprimand thee! These are thy own thoughts, not the words of God. This Meeting House is not a place for thy worldly debates! Save that talk for the hitching post and the watering trough!"

Instantly a dozen people, both men and women, were on their feet, talking at once. Daniel had never seen such an eruption during the worship service. More people stood and joined the debate.

At last, one of the white-haired men came to his feet and pounded on the wooden floor with his cane, bringing the room to an awkward and ringing silence.

"Friends," he said quietly, "this is not seemly. Let us return to our proper manner, lest we be disgraced in the eyes of God."

For a time, the man's words had a calming effect on the assembly.

But then Captain Collins was on his feet again.

"I do not wish to offend anyone," he said simply. "I only want to carry the message that we are small in the eyes of God when we enslave another. I know the West Chester Meeting has already begun a movement to free their African slaves and hire immigrants to work their fields. If we are truly to call ourselves children of God, we cannot shirk our duty to our black brethren. Otherwise how can we hold up our heads and look each other firmly in the eye, knowing that this offensive practice persists in our community?"

Captain Collins took his seat, bowing his head in silence.

Then, as suddenly as it had begun, the service was over, and the elders were shaking hands with one another, a sign that everyone was to do the same and go on their way.

That day, outside the Meeting House, people stood in clusters and talked heatedly. But the Collins family did not take part in the discussions. Elias Collins led his kin home, and they spent the remainder of the day in quiet contemplation.

The following evening, Mainwaring returned and paid the family a cordial visit. Daniel had to admit he brightened the house as soon as he arrived. He joked with the women in the kitchen and always had a cheerful word for everyone. In some ways, he seemed like a long-lost son, returning from a distant journey.

But only Daniel saw what was really happening. Each night, from his window, he could see Mainwaring and Hettie silently meeting and parting. Many young men had flowed through Hettie's life, like water over a dam. But none had spent so much time with her as James Mainwaring.

While this nightly intrigue was taking place in the Quaker household, Captain Collins announced that he was about to leave on another of his month-long voyages to the Caribbean. They had a last family dinner together one evening, and then Captain Collins collected his things and went aboard the *Good Samaritan,* as they would be leaving with the dawn tide.

The next morning, when Daniel looked out into the river channel, where the family ship had been moored, he saw the

Good Samaritan was gone, headed downriver on another expedition.

With the older man out of view, Mainwaring and Hettie became much bolder—and Aunt Terra did nothing to discourage the two. In fact, she fussed over them shamelessly, calling them the most handsome couple in all of Philadelphia, maybe in all of the British Colonies.

One night, shortly after Captain Collins left, Daniel lay awake in the attic on his straw mattress.

Overhead the moon plunged like a sailing ship through wave after wave of grayish clouds. It was a languid evening, with just the suggestion of a breeze. Bored and restless, Daniel rose to his knees and leaned out of the window. He heard the unmistakable sound of Hettie's musical laughter, mixed with the voice of James Mainwaring.

What were they talking about in such urgent tones?

Slipping out of the window, Daniel felt the coolness of the shingles against his palms and the soles of his bare feet. He crabbed down the sloping roof to the sycamore that brushed the back of the house. A short lunge and he was in the arms of the swaying branches, working his way down a set of familiar handholds and footholds until he dropped, as lightly as a cat, on the ground.

Crouching low, Daniel moved in among the boxberry bushes and up to the very edge of the grape arbor. He hid in the shadows.

He waited for his heart to stop racing and for his breathing to become easy and regular. Gathering his courage, he rose slightly in his hiding place and peered through the screen of fronds, into the arbor. There, in the pale moonlight, Daniel could see Hettie, wrapped in the arms of James Mainwaring.

"No, James," Hettie was saying. "What thee ask is impossible."

"But Hedabelle, I am tired of this sneaking around. Besides, I think your aunt would not object. When your uncle returns, I want to be able to speak to him in broad daylight, to ask him for your hand in marriage. Surely I have as much right as those sniveling pups that leer at you on the street."

"Of course thee do," Hettie said, "but thee must consider our public position. We are prominent members of the Friends' Meeting. As long as I am under his roof, Uncle Elias would never permit me to marry a military man."

"Maybe so," Mainwaring said, "but I don't plan to be a military man much longer."

"Oh?" Hettie's voice was bright and sharp in the darkness.

"Listen: I have a plan that will allow me to leave the navy in a few months' time and purchase my own merchant vessel. That will settle your uncle's objections. He might even make me a partner in his shipping business."

"Perhaps. But how?"

"Do you remember my mention of the pirate Jack Scarfield at dinner?" Mainwaring asked.

"Yes, but what of it?"

"Well," Mainwaring said, "Scarfield has become a little too notorious for his own good. I have been approached by a consortium of shipowners who have agreed to finance an expedition to hunt down Scarfield and his crew.

"The investors have been more than generous. They have offered me the command of a heavily armed brig of war, which is right now being outfitted as a pirate-chaser. In two weeks' time, I will leave with a crew of sixty able-bodied men. If all goes well, I will return by summer's end, with Scarfield's head on the point of my sword."

"Uncle Elias will not approve of thy methods," Hettie said.

"Perhaps not. But what about you, Hettie? Would you approve? If I were able to use this opportunity to secure us a bright future, would you despise me?" Mainwaring asked.

"I could never despise thee, James."

"Even if I had Scarfield's blood on my hands?"

"But what if the blood spilled would be thine?"

Mainwaring laughed, taking her hand.

"There is danger, of course, but not as much as you might think," he assured her. "After all, I will have Scarfield out-manned and outgunned. And I will have surprise on my side. That is why I must ask you never to breathe a word of what I have said to anyone. Men's lives depend upon it."

He looked at her. "Hedabelle, will you swear that you love me above all other men?"

"Oh, James. Quakers are not permitted to swear."

"I want to hear the words, Hettie. I want to know that when I return, you will be my wife."

Hettie closed her eyes.

"I swear it, James Mainwaring," she whispered, "I swear

that thee hast captured my heart just as surely as thee will capture the pirate Scarfield."

Mainwaring pulled her to him. They sat embracing in the moonlight.

Then Hettie tore herself away and ran into the house, her dress rustling in the darkness like a dove's wings.

Daniel thought Mainwaring would go then, following the stone path to the garden gate. But he simply stood, his eyes fastened on the back door of the house.

The boy sank into the shadows.

Suddenly, Mainwaring whirled, drew his sword, and sprang like a tiger in Daniel's direction.

The next thing he knew, Daniel was lying on his back with the officer's boot on his chest and the cold blade of the sword laid against the tender skin of his right ear.

Mainwaring peered down and, recognizing Hettie's brother, withdrew the steel and slid his blade into its scabbard.

Then he laughed. It was a light, good-natured laugh, but it made Daniel angry all the same. He had never been attacked so suddenly, and with such violence.

"You young pup," Mainwaring said, ". . . a navy man?

Daniel did not answer. He pulled himself up on one elbow. Instinctively, his hand went to his ear. It was still there.

"How long have you been here?" Mainwaring whispered.

"Long enough," the boy managed. "Long enough to know that you and my sister have a plan."

"We all have secrets," he said. Mainwaring grinned. "Why, even an innocent boy like yourself—"

"You do not need to remind me," Daniel said, drawing himself into a seated position. "But you must admit, you take liberties—"

"I take what I desire," Mainwaring said, "just as any man should. Now, if I were you, I would climb back into my room and stay there. What goes on between your sister and me should not disturb you. In fact, it might even be to your benefit. If all goes well, I will be a merchant captain with my own ship. I will need family members to help me run my ship. Do you follow what I'm saying?"

He offered his hand.

"As one dreamer to another," Mainwaring said, "Shall we swear to be part of each other's future?"

Daniel looked at the officer's hand in the moonlight. But he did not take it. This was too much, too fast.

"I will think on it," he said, rolling to his feet.

"Do not think for long," Mainwaring said, "I leave in two weeks' time."

Daniel didn't answer but walked with quick steps to the sycamore.

A few artful swings and he was up in the branches and crawling back through the attic window.

When he looked down into the garden, he could see that Mainwaring had already left, silently closing the garden gate behind him.

For a long time, Daniel lay on his back on his sleeping mat, staring up at the moon.

The next morning, as he and Tuck were wrestling a

timber into place in the sawpit, Old Man Hinckley appeared at the edge of the pit, looking down at the boys through a haze of sawdust and sunlight. Beside him was the shipmaster, Thomas Greyling.

"What about those two?" Greyling said to Hinckley.

The master carpenter nodded. "They're a little small for what you want."

"No," Greyling said, "I want a pair of boys to do the work in tight spaces." He looked for a moment into Daniel's face, then quickly looked away.

"They'll do," said Hinckley.

"Then get them loaded," Greyling said, making a mark on a paper he held in his hand.

Hinckley motioned to the boys.

"You two. See that boat down there?" He pointed to a longboat tied in the shallows at the edge of the shipyard. Two strong rowers sat in the boat and a dozen of Hinckley's men were already seated in the craft.

"Get aboard her." Hinckley ordered.

"Mister Hinckley, what's this all about?" Tuck asked.

"You can keep your mouth shut, can't you?" Hinckley said.

"Aye, I can. But I only want to know—"

"Get in the boat or you're not going." It was not a threat, just a statement.

The boys shook the sawdust from their clothing and walked down to the boat. It was loaded with men and tools.

"Shove off and do as you're told," Hinckley said to the men.

They pushed off, drifting into the current as the two rowers pulled for the Jersey shore, far in the distance. As they angled through the stiff current, Daniel glanced around at the other men from Hinckley's crew, men he had known for years. It was clear from their expressions that this sudden assignment was a surprise to them all.

"Wonder where we're headed?" one of the men said.

But they didn't have to wonder for long. Once they were on the Jersey side, the longboat pulled into a sheltered eddy behind a small island covered with scrubby, flood-washed growth. Daniel and the others jumped ashore, taking the tools with them.

"What's this all about?" one of the carpenters wondered aloud.

"Only one way to find out," another said, and began to push ahead through the thick underbrush. The others followed.

Upstream, on the hidden side of the island, a strange sight greeted them: Anchored in the shallows, half-hidden by the foliage, was a huge merchant ship. The morning mist was still lifting off the river, hiding its masts and rigging. As the vapors swam up the sides of the hull, Daniel could see a weather-beaten name across the bow. It was the *Mary Anne*.

A big man on the upper deck startled them by throwing down a rope ladder and shouting at them to climb aboard. A few of the men climbed the ladder, carrying the tool bags on their backs. The others scrambled freely up the side of the boat, using the cleats nailed into the hull as footholds.

When Daniel clambered up onto the deck, he caught his

breath. Twenty men were already working there, moving about with great industry. Planking was being laid down to reinforce the deck, and huge cannons were being hoisted into place along the gunwales.

"Now, men," the big man said, "you'll not say a word to anyone about your work here on this ship. You'll not say a word to your wife or your mistress or your mother. Is that clear?"

Hinckley's men nodded.

"If everyone keeps their mouth closed, we can get this ship outfitted and in the water before the town gossips start tellin' everyone from Boston to Barbados that there's a new pirate-chaser cruisin' the coastline. Is that clear?"

Everyone nodded again, more emphatically this time.

"Good. Now, you'll come early and stay late. We have thirteen days to make this ship right and ready for combat. You'll receive double pay for your work here, and if she's ready to sail early, you'll receive a bonus. Any man that wants out, speak up now, and I'll have you rowed back to the yard, no questions asked."

He scanned the rows of men.

"Last chance," he said sternly.

No one moved.

"All right. You're hired for the duration of this project."

He shook his head.

"As you can see, she got shot up pretty bad: pirates, off the coast of Jersey. But underneath all this rubble, she's still a fine two-masted brigantine. Look at her, lads: She's eighty-feet long and weighs one hundred fifty tons, and when she has all of her canvas in the air, I'll daresay she'll do seven knots an hour.

"You'll be giving her a new life, making her into a brig of war. When you're through with her, she'll have twenty cannon and a Long Tom gun pointing out over the bowsprit. But from a distance, she'll look like any other merchant prize."

"But why?" someone asked.

The big man walked over and put his finger on the ship worker's chest.

"Now that's a question you never want to ask, matey. You just do your work and keep your mouth shut."

He jumped on a wooden box, looking down at the crew.

"Enough talk now! There will be grog and food at noon. Go over to the foreman and get your work assignments."

He pointed to a man standing near a pile of lumber, holding a long list in his hand.

As the only boys on the detail, Daniel and Tuck were handed the dirtiest job. They were given iron hammers, hawsing chisels, and baskets of frayed rope fiber and sent down into the darkness of the hold to patch leaks in the hull. By the flickering light of pine-pitch torches, they waded through the knee-deep water and drove the pliable fibers into the beveled joints between the planking, making the hull watertight. From the looks of the boards beneath their feet, this ship had taken a terrible beating in some sea battle.

For the rest of the morning, Daniel and Tuck worked down below, coming up at noon to receive sunlight, air, and a little refreshment.

In the heat of the day, the boys moved away from the others and sat on flat rocks a short distance from the ship, their bare feet dangling in the cold water. They were given grog to drink, just like the older men, and they swallowed the rum and sugar mixture gratefully. They chewed on disks of sailor's hardtack, which Daniel thought tasted like chalk and had the consistency of slate. He used his knife to crack the biscuits into bite-size pieces.

When this meal was finished, Daniel took out his knife and used a smooth river rock to put a new edge on the blade.

Daniel licked his lips.

"Tuck?" he said.

"What is it?" Tuck was cleaning his own knife in the running water.

"Have you ever wondered about the pirates?" Daniel asked. "What their lives are like and such? I mean, it would be adventuresome, wouldn't it?"

"Aye," Tuck said. "But why risk yer neck to the gallows? Most pirates never live to see thirty years. Bein' a common seaman or a carpenter's assistant would be adventure enough. In fact, I plan to say farewell to the shipyard this fall and get a berth on a merchant ship."

Daniel was impressed. "Would your father let you go?"

"Gladly," Tuck said, "Father says I'm a man now and should be off on my own."

"Do you feel like a man?" Daniel asked.

"No," Tuck admitted, "I can't say I do. That's the thing about the sea," he added. "You know you'd be tested."

"That you would," Daniel agreed.

"If I managed to get aboard a ship," Tuck said urgently, "would you go with me and be my shipmate?"

"I don't know that I could, Tuck. It's more complicated for me—"

"Here," Tuck said suddenly, "Let's swear an oath to each other."

"Quakers are not allowed to swear," Daniel said.

But that moment, his hand slipped and his knife sliced into the meat of his right thumb. It was a clean cut, but deep.

Instinctively Daniel leaned forward and thrust his bleeding hand into the river, watching the water turn the color of roses.

"A blood oath," Tuck said. "That's even better."

Tuck drew the blade of his knife across the pad of his thumb. Blood oozed and dripped off the end of his fingers.

"Let's make ourselves a promise," he urged. "Let's swear on our blood that we'll help each other get to sea one day. Will you do that, Daniel?"

Daniel nodded.

Crouching low, Tuck held his hand in the Delaware, letting the current carry the red stain away.

"May I follow my blood downstream," Tuck said.

As if he were making a prayer, Daniel surprised himself by saying, "May I follow my blood downstream, to the sea."

Underwater their hands looked white and clean, like the underside of fish bellies.

"We've sworn it now," Tuck said. "We've sworn it in blood."

Up on deck, the ship's bell was ringing, calling them back to work.

They wrapped their throbbing thumbs in strips of cloth to staunch the bleeding. By the time they were back at work, Daniel knew that his blood was well downstream, on its way to the sea.

CHAPTER FIVE

⌁

*I*N THE DAYS that followed, Daniel and Tuck came to know every corner of the ship. Even though the tasks were menial, Daniel began to take an extraordinary pride in their work. He could see the ship taking shape and returning to its former well-trimmed elegance.

The sail makers started their work the next week, hauling a cloud of canvas up over the deck, poised and ready to catch the wind. The ratlines and lashing spars were set into place, and row after row of short-nosed cannons were positioned on the deck and covered with canvas so the ship could be disguised as a merchant.

The next day, when the boys came to work, they saw that the name of the *Mary Anne* had been scraped from the bow and a new name had been painted in bold blue letters.

The vessel was now called the *Sea Turtle*. A docile name. But like a turtle, Daniel thought, the ship held a great deal concealed beneath its innocent-looking shell.

Because they had finished their work on the ship's hull, the boys were given an assignment on the upper deck, in the open air. The outer wall of the captain's cabin had been smashed to splinters by what looked to be cannonballs or perhaps a fallen mast. The boys were instructed to tear away the wreckage and use fresh planking to build a solid wall in its place.

While they were tearing away the shattered boards, Daniel ducked inside the cabin. Its walls were paneled with rich blond wood, highlighted with sparkling brass. There was an ample-sized bunk in one corner, a writing desk, and a place for maps and charts to be hung on the wall. One amazing feature was a compass set into the ceiling above the captain's bunk so that he could check the ship's course without even leaving the warmth of his bed.

But the thing that interested Daniel most was the officer's closet. It was separated from the room by a double set of louvered doors. Standing behind the doors, Daniel discovered that he could peer through the slanting slats and see clearly into the room. He realized that a person could hide behind these doors and see everything, without being discovered.

A wild plan sprang into his mind. Could he stow away on the ship by hiding in the captain's closet? No, Daniel thought, that would be too obvious. What if someone besides Mainwaring should discover him? And how would he get inside the closet in the first place?

But as they were working on the outer wall, another idea, one more artful and intricate, settled like a bird on his shoulder. He considered it for a full hour before he decided to go ahead.

Daniel noticed a space of four feet between the cabin's

closet doors and the outer wall. It occurred to him that he and Tuck could easily build a false wall into the back of the closet, creating a closet two feet deep and a secret compartment two feet wide, which Daniel could enter and exit through a loose board on the outer wall. Daniel felt certain it would work, but he also knew he would need Tuck's help. That meant telling him everything.

That afternoon, Daniel drew Tuck aside and told him about his plans for the secret compartment.

After he had finished, Tuck gave a low whistle.

"I must admit," the boy said, "I always took you for a bit of a sissy. But this is a bold plan, Daniel. Even I wouldn't have thought of this, not in a hundred years. I'm feelin' a little sad that I won't be goin' with you. But, look, I'll get over that real quick. I got my own plans, as you know. But you're ready now, huh?"

Daniel nodded.

Tuck clapped him on the shoulder.

"Don't let anyone ever say that Tuck O'Neil went back on a blood promise. I'll do whatever I can to help you, mate. I just got one question."

"Go ahead."

"Aren't you a bit worried about how you're gonna survive in this tiny space? I mean, it'll be like layin' in a coffin."

Daniel shook his head. "I already thought of that. I only need to stay in there the first night, until the ship is out to sea. Then I can slide the outside board away and present myself to Mainwaring. Once he sees that I came aboard of my own free will, I think he'll make me a member of the crew."

Tuck looked doubtful.

"What if he changes his mind and puts you ashore somewhere in Jersey and you have to spend the next week walking back through the Pine Barrens?"

"Come on." Daniel grinned. "I thought you were looking for adventure."

Tuck glanced downriver. "All right, Daniel. You won me over. But God help us if Old Man Hinckley finds out. He'll skin us alive."

Daniel grinned. "Don't worry," he said, "Hinckley won't find out."

The building of Daniel's hiding place went beautifully. It took two days to get everything fitted just right. They managed to engineer a foot-wide board on the outer wall with holes drilled in it so Daniel could breathe and keep an eye on the upper deck. The board would slide away from inside so he could show himself when he felt the time was right. In the next several days, they smuggled aboard a water bottle, a sack of biscuits, a chamber pot, and a scrap of blanket, safely stowing them in the secret hideaway. Thankfully there was so much work for the crew no one paid the slightest attention to what they were doing.

The day after the compartment was finished, Mainwaring himself came aboard for an inspection of the ship. Daniel slipped down into the hold, looking busy and staying out of sight.

In the evenings, when the officer called at his uncle's house, Daniel made it a point to avoid even seeing him.

But then he realized, with the many details of preparing for the voyage, there would scarcely be room in Mainwaring's thoughts for Daniel. Besides, the young officer was in love with Hettie. And that was enough to occupy the mind of any man.

At last, the job was finished. The *Sea Turtle* would slip away with the morning tide on the morning of July fourth. On the evening of July second, Daniel slept poorly.

The next morning, he told Terra he had been given a special assignment and would be staying down at the shipyard for a few weeks.

She scarcely looked at him when she said, "Fine, then. I'll not wait up for thee." When he left after breakfast, Hettie ignored him completely.

It was a fine day, hot but clear, and the work went well.

Tuck waited until quitting time before sealing Daniel up in his concealed compartment.

The crew had already begun to arrive and there was a great deal of confusion on deck, so Daniel was not worried about being missed on the return boat.

Once Daniel was safely stowed, Tuck reached in through the opening.

"Good seafarin' to you," he said, shaking Daniel's hand. "Maybe we'll see each other again soon."

"I hope so," Daniel said, grinning in the dark. "Thanks for keeping your promise."

Then Tuck slid the board shut, and Daniel was swallowed by the hot, close darkness. For the next hour or two, he listened to every sound on the deck, fearful he might be discovered. But at last, his fears lessened, and he settled into the relative comfort of his compartment. Later that evening, he heard Mainwaring's voice, heard him enter the cabin and listened with some satisfaction as the officer placed his clothing into the closet Daniel had built for him.

Then he closed his eyes and slept his last night within sight of dry land.

CHAPTER SIX

$\overbrace{\hspace{2cm}}$

*D*ANIEL WAS SICK, sick in a way that he had never been sick before.

The first night, he had been all right in the confined space. While the crew was making preparations, he had slept soundly, waking only at dawn when he heard the anchor being raised and felt the ship being rowed out into the river current. They were swept off downstream with a gentle rocking motion.

But sometime during that first day on the water, Daniel began to feel a strange queasiness in the pit of his stomach. At first, he thought he might simply be hungry, so he took a little of the bread and water he had brought with him. But the feeling didn't go away. It grew worse.

The gentle rocking of the boat, which had been so soothing, had now become annoying. As the downstream current pulled the *Sea Turtle* toward the ocean, Daniel was tossed around in the hot, confined space like a brass bead in a wooden cup. He fixed his eyes to the holes in the outer wall and saw the shore slipping by at a dizzying speed.

The constant motion made his eyes throb and his inner ears ache with a dull pain. Hoping for some relief, Daniel rolled onto all fours and crawled across the dimly lit space to the far corner where he had stored his clay chamber pot.

Bracing himself against the swaying wall, he bent over the pot, closed his eyes, and waited. Down in the innermost depths of his stomach, a violent trembling began. Daniel pitched forward, opening his mouth wide, and watched through teary eyes as his ration of bread and water fell splashing into the pot.

For a moment, his airway was blocked and he almost panicked, thinking that he wouldn't be able to catch his breath. But at last, he was able to swallow and draw a long sobbing breath. He coughed pitifully, wiping the vomit from his face and neck with his hands. He worried that the sounds of his struggle might carry into the cabin, where he heard voices faintly, as if from another world.

To make matters worse, when he tried to crawl back to his sleeping place, his foot caught the edge of the chamber pot and upset it, spilling the putrid liquid all over the floor of the compartment. He tried to mop it up with his sleeve. But it was no use. The floor, and everything on it, was soaked. With a groan, he lay down in the sodden blankets and tried to sleep. This was how Daniel spent his second night on the water.

In the morning, he rose with the familiar queasy feeling and peered through the eyeholes. He was shocked to discover that they were at sea. During the night, they had passed down the Delaware River, out the mouth of the Delaware Bay, and at last into the great Atlantic Ocean.

Even in his ignoble condition, Daniel felt an indescribable delight as he crouched in his chamber, surveying, for the very first time, the unbroken horizon. Up until this moment, he had never seen a body of water he couldn't swim across, and now here he was, running his eyes over the clean blue line that stretched over the very curve of the earth.

But his elation didn't last for long. Now that they were in the open seas, the boat didn't just rock back and forth, it pitched and plunged and rolled.

Bracing his legs against the sidewall, Daniel lay back in his filthy blankets and tried to sleep. But sleep wouldn't come. Instead he fell into a delirium. His body was bathed in sweat, and then he was overcome with a convulsion of chills. Images of sailing ships and pirate crews danced through his brain while bright colors flashed like cannon fire in the darkness behind his eyeballs.

At last, on the evening of his second day in the chamber, Daniel rose from his blankets filled with a feeling of disgust. He had had enough of this tight, cramped compartment. He felt if he had to inhale one more breath of the moist, putrid air, he would go mad.

Now was the time to free himself from his confinement and face whatever consequences awaited him. He groped along the darkened wall until his fingers closed around the edge of the panel that would slide aside, allowing him to crawl out onto the open deck. He pushed, but the board did not move. He knelt, bracing himself against the wall, and worked his fingers underneath the edge of the board, pushing until he thought the blood vessels in his neck would pop. But still the board did not move.

Bending down and peering through the eye slits, Daniel saw something he had not seen before: Apparently some handy soul had rolled a heavy barrel up against the outer wall and lashed it into place.

Daniel knew there was no way he could shove the barrel aside. He was trapped. He would have to break through the back wall of Mainwaring's closet and crawl out into the captain's cabin. It was not a good solution, but it was the only one Daniel could devise.

Daniel searched through his meager belongings and found his carpenter's knife. Thrusting the blade in between the boards, he began to work them loose. The nails gave off a sharp squeaking sound as he pried back one board.

Daniel heard the scraping of chair legs on the floor in the captain's cabin. Setting his ear to the opening he had made, he heard muffled voices. He laid aside his knife and reared back, putting his foot through the board. It shattered into a dozen pieces.

Lantern light streamed into the closet as Daniel ducked through the hole and found himself among a forest of hanging clothes. Groping about, he pushed the louvered doors aside and crawled headfirst into the lighted room.

Daniel glanced up. There, under the swaying lantern, he could make out the astonished faces of Mainwaring and three of his officers. Caught in the middle of their dinner, they had sprung to their feet and drawn their pistols.

Daniel grinned sheepishly at Mainwaring, suddenly aware of how ill kempt he must look, with his vomit-splattered clothing and his fever-wet hair plastered to his forehead. He remained on all fours, like a wild beast.

"Hello," Daniel said.

Mainwaring lowered the pistol. Daniel had just time to see a light of recognition dawn in the captain's eyes before a powerful spasm overtook him. He rose, and reaching for the back of a chair to steady himself, he pitched forward, then stumbled and heaved, throwing a fresh cascade of vomit onto all four officers.

The men began shouting in disgust, trying to flick the offensive clots from their clothing. But Daniel couldn't hear them. His legs turned to jelly, and he slumped to the floor, limp as a rag doll left out in the rain.

When Daniel woke, he found himself dressed in clean canvas clothing, lying in a swinging canvas hammock, somewhere in the depths of the ship. The feeble flame of a yellowed candle cast an eerie light on the walls.

As soon as he opened his crusted eyes, he heard a voice at the door saying, "Send for the captain, the boy's coming around."

Daniel closed his eyes and waited.

A few moments later, Mainwaring appeared. He had put away his dashing uniform and was dressed in common seaman's clothing, no different from the rest of the crew.

"Well, Daniel," Mainwaring began, "you have had the honor of throwing up on some of the best people in the Royal Navy. That is a distinction very few boys your age can claim."

Even though his tone was stern, Daniel could see that

Mainwaring's eyes were dancing with a mischievous light.

Daniel began to sit up in the hammock, but the contraption swung awkwardly, threatening to dump him on the floor. So he lay back, trying to remain as still as possible.

"I only wanted to go to sea," Daniel said wearily.

"Well, you've done it," Mainwaring said. "As I'm sure you know, you have placed me in a very awkward situation."

"I know that," Daniel said.

"We may be disguised as a merchant trader," Mainwaring said, "but this is a combat vessel. And I have every intention of giving Scarfield the fight of his life. I am sure he will not go down easily. I know I will lose some men during this expedition. I cannot allow you to be among them. If you should be killed or maimed, your family would never forgive me."

"I doubt I would be missed," Daniel said.

Mainwaring shook his head.

"You might be surprised," he said. "Both Hettie and Mrs. Collins told me privately they were afraid you would someday slip away to sea and meet the same fate as your father."

Daniel struggled to sit up in his hammock. "They told you that?"

"Yes, Daniel. You have a fine family. And with any luck, I will return you safely to them in a few weeks' time. Then, when your sister and I have completed our nuptials, you will no doubt be seeing a good deal of me.

"But for now, the men aboard this floating fortress are your family. As the captain of the ship, I am like a father, personally responsible for the life of every man aboard. And your sudden appearance in our midst has not lessened my burden."

"I'll try to be useful," Daniel said.

"I'm sure you will. I cannot take time from my own duties to attend to your welfare so I have assigned you to the ship's carpenter, Mr. Killington. You will be under his care for the duration of the voyage. You will do exactly as he says. Is that understood?"

"Yes, sir."

"Good. And I would refrain from discussing your family connections with any member of the crew. Is that clear?"

"Yes, sir."

Mainwaring stood and turned to leave.

"By the way," he said jauntily, "when the cannonballs start to fly, don't try to be a hero. Many a foolish man lost his head just before he lost his head."

"Yes, sir," Daniel repeated.

Mainwaring leaned out into the passageway.

"Mister Killington, you may come in now," he said. Then he was gone.

A small, wiry man appeared in the doorway. The first thing Daniel noticed was that he was unusually hairy—with bristly hair sprouting from his nose and ears and curling up from his open shirt collar. He had a stiff beard and eyebrows so thick they grew together in the center of his forehead. Through the thick hair of his forearms, Daniel could make out the blue stains of nautical tattoos. He was holding a steaming tin cup of what smelled like cider.

Daniel rose slightly and offered his hand. "Hello, Mr.

Killington," he said weakly.

Killington looked down at the boy's hand as if it were a piece of garbage.

"Put that hand away," the carpenter said sourly. He was not an old man, no more than middle-aged, but his voice was raspy and storm-beaten.

"There will be no handshaking on this ship," he said, "and no saluting or bowing or other such pleasantries. This is not one of your Quakerly Meetings. Why have you come sneaking and sniveling aboard this ship?"

Daniel hung his head.

"I guess I came for adventure," he said uncertainly.

"Adventure! Great God in Heaven!" Killington declared. "You'll find no adventure on this ship, you cabbage-head! Only backbreaking work and wormy biscuits and the worst boredom the world has to offer. Why, I'll work you until you're sorry you ever left your mama's lap!"

Daniel was about to point out that his mother was dead. But the carpenter gave him no chance.

"This is not a pleasure cruise, you laggard, you dolt-head, you sorry piece of goat dung! If I had any sense at all, I'd toss you overboard right now and be done with it!"

Daniel was silent. He had never been spoken to in such a rough manner, even at the shipyard.

"I swear," the carpenter ranted, "if the ship were manned with nothing but dreamy-eyed lads such as yourself, we would be shipwrecked before we even caught sight of pirates!"

He sighed mightily. "I don't know what is between you

and the captain—and I don't want to know. All I know is he has ordered me to take you under my wing and make sure you don't get yourself killed. So let's begin the sorry task: What do you call yourself?"

"Daniel."

Killington nodded.

"Not a bad name," he said, "but I will call you Dan. This will save me a breath each time I speak to you."

"Yes, sir."

"Don't be calling me 'sir'," he said tersely. "You will call me Killy, just as all the others do."

"Yes, Killy."

"Right enough. Now get up from that sling and do your duty: Move smartly now! Take this mug of hot cider up to the lookout—and be quick about it. And don't spill a single drop, or the jack tar in the crow's nest will give you a cuff on the ear. He's mighty particular about his cider. Report to me on the quarter-deck when you are done."

Then he vanished, leaving the steaming cup of amber liquid sitting on a shelf by the doorway. All was silent and creaking. Overhead Daniel could hear the muffled sounds of men working on the deck.

Daniel rose slightly. His head felt like a pumpkin; it was all he could do to hold it upright. Gingerly he lowered his bare feet to the floor and attempted to stand. He stumbled and fell, catching himself on the hammock rope. The tiny cabin was a whirl of muddy colors. He closed his eyes and willed the room to stop its spinning. After several long breaths, things settled a little.

He walked to the doorway on feet that did not seem to belong to him. Daniel hooked his fingers into the cup's crude, metal handle. He had to hold it carefully because the tin was scalding hot.

Daniel staggered out onto the gangway and crawled up the steep steps to the open deck. He was still very dizzy.

The sky was impossibly blue, studded with clouds and alive with flocks of gulls. Everything was plunging and creaking and swaying to the sickening heartbeat of the ocean waves. The taut sails hummed in the wind.

No one seemed to be paying the least attention to him. Everywhere men were shouting and climbing and hauling at ropes.

He looked around and saw Mainwaring on the upper deck. Daniel raised his hand to wave, but the captain was looking far out to sea.

Just then, he heard Killy's voice, over his left shoulder.

"Didn't I tell you to take that cider up to the lookout?" the carpenter shouted.

"Yes," Daniel said, "but I don't know how to get up there."

"You son of a pig's snout!" Killy swore. "Were you born stupid? Look above you, you blockhead. Do you see that long pole-lookin' thing there? That piece of a tree? That's the mast.

"Well, you go up the rigging—that rope ladder there— and when you get to the lookout's perch—you'll be fifty feet above the deck by then—you give the man his cider. Now shake a leg! His drink's getting cold, and there's nothing a man hates more than cold cider."

Daniel tilted his head back and squinted into the glare of the morning sun. Far above him, he could make out a sailor in a red-striped shirt standing on a small platform attached to the main mast.

"Now, up you go!" Killy was saying, "And remember: One hand for you and one for the ship. Don't let loose of a handhold until you've got a death grip on the next one. Is that clear?"

Daniel was about to ask how he was supposed to do that while he was carrying the cider. But something in Killy's glowering expression told him to shut up and climb.

Daniel tilted his head back. The top of the mast seemed far, far above him, almost disappearing into the clouds.

He swallowed. There was nothing to do but climb. He pulled himself up onto the rigging, steadying the cup in one hand. But the rigging swayed and shook beneath him, and he spilled most of the scalding liquid within the first ten feet. He paused and clung to the rope lines. His breath was coming in fast, shallow gasps. This was much more dangerous than the rooftops of Spruce Street.

Below him, the spangled ocean heaved and plunged. His eyes fixed on the moving surface of the water, and he almost lost his balance and fell. But then he forced himself to arch his head back and look at the sun-washed world up above.

Although his head was spinning, he was climbing, much as he had climbed the old sycamore behind the house on Spruce Street. He was climbing, up above the human world, into a space of wind and rope and heaving canvas, where only birds and angels and hearty sailors go.

Daniel did not look down, not even once, until he was just below the level of the crow's nest. Then he stole a glance between his bare feet and was horrified to see that the ship was not upright, as he imagined it would be. Instead it was canted to the side, running hard before the wind, and there was nothing below him but swelling, fast-moving water. The ship looked very small, like a chip of wood tossed on the surface of the vast, vast ocean. Suddenly nothing made sense; the sky and the ship were not where they were supposed to be; the horizon was striking off at a crazy angle.

The wind pulled at Daniel, filling his billowing shirt and threatening to tear him from the rigging. He clutched tight to the rope ladder. As he did, his fingers spasmed. Then, before he could do anything about it, the tin cup slipped from his grasp. He watched it tumble and fall, end over end, for an impossibly long time before it plopped into the racing ocean—gone.

He groaned aloud. He had failed. Now he would get a beating.

In his entire life, no one had ever struck him in anger. But those days were over, he knew. Now he was out in the bare-knuckled, bloody-nosed world, where there was no time for quiet reflection or holy conversation.

Tears of frustration started up in his eyes. They must not see him cry. Daniel knew that. But he could not stop himself. He was afraid. He was afraid and alone and had gotten himself wrapped up in something that was far, far beyond him. And there wasn't a thing he could do about it.

CHAPTER SEVEN

*A*LL AT ONCE, something clutched at the back of his shirt collar, and he felt himself being hauled upward. A moment later, he was lying on his back on the wooden look-out platform. Standing over him was a sunburned sailor in a striped shirt.

"Hold on there," the seaman was shouting. "Where's my cider? I'm powerful thirsty!" He was grinning from ear to ear.

Daniel steadied himself against the wooden planks and crabbed his way over to place his back against the mast. The platform itself was made up of narrow slats of wood with gaping spaces between them. He drew a deep, shuddering breath. All around him, the horizon dipped and plunged. He closed his eyes and tried to steady himself. But the whole world was moving, with a maddening, unstoppable rhythm.

"Where's my cider?" the sailor repeated.

Daniel couldn't answer. He felt empty inside, as if the wind had ripped everything from him.

Then he felt the sailor's long fingers, resting on his head. Daniel flinched. But when he sensed that the man did not mean to strike him, he looked up.

"It's not as bad as all that," the lookout shouted. He was not much larger than Daniel, but much older. But he seemed to be a different kind of creature, like a bird, clinging to the rigging as casually as a swallow in a storm.

"I spilled your cider," Daniel admitted.

"Forget the cider," the fellow shouted. "Even a jungle monkey couldn't have made that climb without spilling the whole thing!"

He clapped Daniel on the shoulder.

"You did tolerably well, lad. A lot of the greenhorns never make it up the riggin'. I've seen some of 'em freeze to the lines and cry for their mamas. Others have to be lowered down by a rope.

"Why, Old Killy was just testing you—to see what you are made of. You shoulda seen the things the old-timers made me do when I first came aboard. Before you know it, you'll be swinging around these shrouds like a long-armed baboon!"

Daniel threw a glance downward and saw Killy, far below, standing with his head thrown back and his hands on his hips, watching.

Daniel sighed. He remembered a similar incident, on the first day he reported to the shipyard, when the dock workers sent him on a wild-goose chase all over the yard, looking for a mythical tool called a left-handed smoke turner.

He was beginning to feel a little better about his climb.

"Before you go down," the lookout said, sweeping his hand across the horizon, "take a look yonder. Ever seen a view like this?"

It was true. Daniel had never seen anything quite like it. It was vast, beyond anything he could have imagined.

The lookout pointed with his chin to the west.

"You can't see it," he shouted above the wind, "but that's the Virginia coastline over there. We'll be following the trade winds south. All the merchants come this way, headed to the Carolinas, then on to the Caribbean Islands!"

Daniel took in a deep breath. This was something grand—to have the world spread out below and a strong wind to carry you to distant lands. Suddenly the inland world of wheat fields and stone-covered streets seemed slow and cloddish.

"You best get down," the lookout said. "Killy will give you an earful about dropping the cup. But don't let it worry you. If you keep your nerve and don't complain, he'll slack off and you'll be treated like a reg'lar jack tar!"

He held out his hand.

"Charley Boatknife's my name," he declared. "What's your'n?"

"Daniel—Daniel Collins."

"Well, good to know ya, lad. Now get yourself back down there before Killy busts a gut."

Daniel nodded and lowered himself through the hole in the platform. Going down was far easier than going up, now that he was free of the blasted cup and could use both his hands and his feet.

In a few moments, he was stepping down out of the shrouds, feeling the firmness of the deck beneath his feet.

Killy was shouting in his ear.

"You clodhopper! What was that business with the cup? You'll have to pay for that, y'know! It'll come outta your share, sure enough!"

Daniel said nothing, wiping his wet hands on the front of his shirt.

Far overhead, he could see the lookout, clinging nimbly to the lines, looking at something far out to sea. Daniel realized he had not even thought to thank him for his encouraging words.

Killington peered into his face.

"How do you feel?" he asked.

"Three-quarters dead," Daniel admitted.

"Aye, the seasickness," Killy said. "At first, you're afraid you're going to die. Then you're afraid you won't."

He laughed at his own joke.

At the moment, Daniel didn't see much humor in the comment, but he smiled weakly anyway.

Killy reached down and cupped his hands around a tankard of dark liquid.

"Here," he offered. "Take a sip of this."

"What is it?"

"Seasickness cure. I had the cook make it up for you."

"What's in it?" Daniel asked, taking the heavy container in his hands and sniffing at it cautiously.

"You don't want to know," Killy said. "Just drink it down."

Daniel closed his shaking hands around the concoction and lifted it to his lips.

It went down better than he had anticipated, tasting thick

and sweet. Killy stood patiently by and watched as the boy drained the tankard and handed it back. Then the carpenter nodded.

"Spend as much time in the open air as you can," he advised. "When the heaves come, go to the leeward side and spill your guts over the railing. If it comes out the other end, use the latrine up there in the bow of the ship. You've got to get the last of that land food out of your system. Then you'll be fit as a fiddle and ready for some proper food: hardtack and salt beef and maybe even a spot of grog."

"Grog?"

"Aye, boy. All the proper seamen drink it. Just what a man needs to get him through the rough days at sea."

Daniel groaned. Something was coming up. He stumbled toward the side of the ship and leaned himself across the railing, heaving until he was empty. When he was finished, he looked around for Killy. But the carpenter was gone, leaving him to work out his stomach troubles on his own.

It took Daniel two days to go through the seasickness cure, drinking a tankardful twice a day. At night, he lay in his hammock in the carpenter's small cabin below decks, periodically emptying himself until he thought he would turn inside out.

Then, one day, he woke and noticed something miraculous: The seething in his stomach and the pounding in his head were gone. He swung his feet to the floor and stood, feeling in full possession of his senses.

Daniel walked on sure legs up into the salt air and the

sunlight. He felt reborn. Suddenly the deck of the ship, which had seemed so loathsome before, was an appealing place, sparkling with morning sun, filled with the shouting and scurrying of the crew. The day was blue and full of promise, no sight of land, only hills and valleys of ocean waves, as far as the eye could see. Colorful flags were snapping in the breeze overhead.

"There you are," Killy sang out, "walking like a proper seaman! Come and set for a while."

The carpenter was brushing a handful of wood shavings off a barrel lashed down under the mast. They sat in the shade of the great sail.

"Now, Dan," Killy said, "we may find ourselves in combat with the pirates this very afternoon, and there are a few things you must know."

"The *Sea Turtle* carries about one hundred men," he began, "and each man must know how he fits into the crew. Lookee here . . ."

He crouched down and drew a pyramid on the wet deck with his finger.

"Captain Mainwaring is up here at the top," he began.

Daniel wrinkled his forehead.

"I thought he was a lieutenant," he said.

"In the regular navy he surely is," Killy admitted, "but aboard this ship he is the captain, and you will address him as such. His powers are absolute and his word is law. He charts our course and commands the ship during battle.

"You must never speak directly to the captain unless he speaks to you. Instead you speak to him through his officers.

But being as how you've thrown up on them, I wouldn't go out of my way to speak with them either."

"You know about that?" Daniel asked, his face reddening.

"Aye, the whole ship knows by now. Many an enlisted man has wished he could do the same from time to time."

Killy returned to his drawing.

"Underneath the captain is the first mate, Mr. Buckthorn. He's the one over there on the upper deck with the bushy sideburns. Mr. Buckthorn is responsible for the day-to-day running of the ship. In the terrible event that the captain would be wounded or killed, Mr. Buckthorn would take command.

"Under Mr. Buckthorn is the boatswain, Mr. Hibbington. He pipes the men to work and manages the upkeep of the rigging and the maneuvering of the sails. He commands the evening watch.

"Duty is divided into six watches of four hours each. Half the sailing crew stands each watch. One group takes two watches at night so that every other night the men will get a full night's sleep. You and I do not stand watch.

"As to the sailors themselves, there are two kinds: The able seamen are experienced hands who can do whatever is required to run the ship. They can go aloft and unfurl a top-sail in a strong wind or take their turn at the capstan, raising the anchor. Below them are the ordinary seamen, still learning the trade. This ship carries sixteen able seamen and twenty-four ordinary sailors.

"There are a few other specialists among the crew: The cook is called Dr. Bones and, I will admit, brings no special qualifications to the job. We have a sail maker, who sees to the stitching and repairing of the canvas. There is a quartermaster who keeps the gear; an armorer who takes charge of the weapons; and a surgeon, Dr. Esquemeling. Sometimes we carpenters are called upon to help the doctor in his operations."

"Why?"

"Because," Killy said, "we have the saws."

Daniel felt a queasy feeling in the pit of his stomach. "How about the cannons?" he asked, changing the subject.

"All right. I'm comin' to that. This vessel carries ten cannons. They fire a six-pound cannonball. That's heavy enough to knock a hole the size of a melon in a pirate ship. It takes at least four men to load, fire, and clean the cannon.

"Besides the gunnery crew, we also have a detachment of twenty-four marines, sharpshooters, and swordsmen who can direct musket fire or storm aboard an enemy ship. Any questions so far?" Killy asked.

Daniel shook his head. Actually he had a hundred questions. But something told him that this was the time to listen, not to talk.

"Now, how do we fit into all this?" Killy asked.

"We keep the water out, I guess."

Killy smiled. "A good answer. It's a wooden world, and a ship's carpenter could be kept busy morning to night just patching the leaks and seeing to the masts and spars.

"But on a combat vessel, the work becomes much more urgent. Sometimes, after a battle, the masts and rigging will be laying about the deck like toppled trees. Sometimes the hull will be sprouting leaks from a dozen places, each one threatening to sink the ship. It's then we need to set to and make things right."

Daniel nodded, trying to imagine the urgency of doing carpentry on a sinking ship.

"Lastly, but just as important," Killy said, "we carpenters are the firefighters. When you hear the cry 'Battle stations,' we report to the upper deck with our water buckets and our wet blankets.

"One other thing: You've seen that tin-covered cabinet by our quarters down in the hold?"

"Yes."

"That's the powder magazine. All the gunpowder on board is kept in there. Fire must not touch it. If it does, the whole ship'll go up in an explosion that will rattle the teeth of the angels in Heaven. If a fire starts there, we have to snuff it out— and quick! Otherwise, the ship is lost."

Daniel swallowed hard.

"Now, if the worst should happen and the ship starts to sink, don't panic. Just head for one of the lifeboats and get yourself into the water as quickly as you can. If you get swept overboard, don't waste your breath yelling for help. No one will hear you. Instead just swim the best you can. By the way, you can swim can't you?"

"Yes," Daniel said, "I learned to swim in the Delaware River."

"Well enough. You'd be surprised how many sailors can't swim a stroke. You turn your back to the waves and keep your head above water. Raise your arm every now and again to mark your position. When the smoke clears, someone will be along in a boat to pick you up. If you can catch on to a floating piece of wood, so much the better.

"Now, here's a question: What is the worst danger you face in a naval battle?"

Daniel thought for a moment.

"Being struck by a cannonball?" he ventured.

Killy shook his head.

"Chances of that are rare. To be honest, the cannon is not an accurate weapon and most gunners are miserable shots. No, boy, the worst danger in a naval battle is splinters."

"Splinters?"

"Aye. Fractured wood. When a cannonball strikes the hull, it sends a shower of splinters into the air."

Killy pulled up his shirt and showed a festering wound in his side, just below the last rib.

"See that? Got those splinters in battle off the coast of Venezuela two months ago, and the wound is still devilin' me. Being a carpenter, you've had a splinter in your finger, haven't you?"

Daniel nodded.

"You know how that thin sliver of wood can swell and fester and torture you? Well, picture yourself shot through with hundreds of them. When the cannonballs start to fly, keep your head down. The air'll be filled with a hailstorm of flying splinters, and if you catch a mouthful, you'll be sorry."

Daniel nodded.

Killy reached into a canvas bag at his feet and drew out a long-barreled flintlock pistol and a two-foot long sword in a wooden sheath.

"In the unlikely event that we are boarded by a pirate crew, you'll need these. Have you ever fired a pistol or used a sword?"

"No," Daniel said, "I come from a Quaker household. Weapons are forbidden."

Killy wrinkled his brow. "I daresay, when a pirate comes over that railing with a knife in his teeth and a pistol in each hand, you'll find a wealth of comfort in knowing you can defend yourself. Leave the fighting to the marines and the gunnery crew. If we are boarded, just get your back up against something and use the pistol and the sword to keep the devils away from you.

"I want you to practice loading this handpiece until you can do it in your sleep. Here's a flask of gunpowder and the ramrod, and the blade."

Daniel tentatively reached out for the pistol, knowing he was holding a dangerous, forbidden object. It was heavy and beautiful, at the same time. A belt clip allowed him to carry it whenever he was on deck. He drew the short sword from its scabbard and glanced at the edge. It was razor-sharp.

"Any questions?" Killy was asking.

"Yes," Daniel said, replacing the sword in its scabbard. "When do we eat?"

Killy clapped him on the shoulder and laughed, "Aye, you must be feelin' better! We eat next at six bells. The bell's rung to call us to mess. Then Dr. Bones will fill you with some proper grub."

Daniel was looking forward to that. But before he could

conjure up a real hunger, the man in the crow's nest, far overhead, sang out, "Smoke to the southwest!"

Daniel glanced up and, sure enough, there on the horizon, a cloud of smoke billowed up into the sky.

He heard the cry, "Battle stations!"

The entire crew sprang to action.

"Come along," Killy said. "We'll see to those water buckets."

While they were laying out their firefighting gear, a seaman climbed into the rigging overhead, ready to adjust the sails.

The gunnery crew rolled back their cannons and laid their shot and powder ready. The marines scrambled for their muskets and ran up onto the deck, taking their places along the railings.

Daniel could see Captain Mainwaring on the upper deck, standing at the rail with a long spyglass. Every eye was trained on the cloud in the distance.

Then Daniel glimpsed a ship in the distance.

She was a frigate, a merchant. And she was afire. As they drew closer, he could see the yellow flames leaping on her deck. Her mast and rigging were in ruins; her sails hung useless, torn to blackened shreds.

Then Daniel saw many dark objects, floating half-submerged all about the sinking ship: bodies.

"God in Heaven help us," Killy muttered. "It's the work of pirates, sure enough."

"What do we do?" Daniel asked.

"Nothin' we can do, lad. The pirates have done their

worst and moved on, leavin' only the dead behind."

But not all of the sad crew were dead.

Overhead, the lookout shouted, "Man on the deck!"

Daniel narrowed his eyes in the sharp sunlight. And indeed there was one man left alive, tied to the mast. He was slumped forward, rolling his head from side to side, as if fighting to stay conscious. He was wearing a captain's great-coat that was stained with blood. On his chest, a white placard flapped in the breeze.

Mainwaring ordered a boat lowered and sent Mr. Hibbington and a dozen marines over to rescue the poor man.

The entire crew watched as the longboat rowed over. The marines scrambled aboard the burning ship, quickly cut the man away from the mast, and lowered him into their boat.

Moments later, a dozen hands were lifting the wounded man up onto the upper deck. They laid him out at Mainwaring's feet. Everyone crowded around, staring. Dr. Esquemeling, looking distinguished in a long coat, bent over the unfortunate captain. He plucked a bottle of whiskey from his medical bag, uncorked it and touched it to the man's lips. The wounded man drank gratefully.

"Stand back now," the surgeon ordered. "Give him air, for God's sake!"

The crew moved off a respectful distance.

Daniel stood, watching as the doctor pulled a razor from his pocket and used it to cut the buttons off the man's coat. He lifted the flaps aside, then opened his shirt. From where he stood, Daniel could see that the glistening digestive organs of his lower belly were exposed to the open air.

Dr. Esquemeling looked up at Mainwaring and shook his head. The wounded man began trembling violently then, his feet and hands drumming on the wooden deck, beating out a weird, irregular cadence. A death rattle began working its way up his throat.

Then the man's eyes rolled up into his head, and he lay still.

Mr. Hibbington handed Mainwaring a square of paper.

"Sir, you will want to see this. It was pinned to the poor man's chest."

Mainwaring looked down at the paper, and Daniel saw his jaws tighten. The captain handed the paper back to Hibbington.

"Read it to the crew," he ordered.

Mister Hibbington looked doubtful. But when the captain nodded, the boatswain stepped up into the rigging and read the message in a clear voice.

"To Captain James Mainwaring—

"Beware: I look forward to meeting you, face to face. You may find me by following the trail of smoking wreckage. I hope you like your meat well-cooked. Because that is how you shall have it."

There was an uncomfortable silence.

Hibbington cleared his throat.

"It is signed Captain Jack Scarfield."

Mainwaring swung up into the rigging, where everyone could see him.

"Men," he said, "it would appear that Captain Scarfield

wants to play a game of hide-and-seek. These pirates are like children. They invent games to amuse themselves while innocent people die horrible deaths! I can not tolerate it!

"I will follow this pirate all the way to the Caribbean, if need be. But, I promise you, we will find him. And when we do, it is his meat that will be cooked!"

Hibbington drew his sword and thrust it, point upward, at the sky.

"What do you say, shipmates? Are we with the captain?"

The crew roared.

"Thank you, men," Mainwaring said. "You're a fine crew. Mr. Hibbington, trim the sails. We have a pirate to catch!"

The crew cheered again and sprang about their work.

The dead man lay forgotten, his blood making a shimmering puddle on the deck.

Daniel tore his eyes away. He lifted his face to the sun. The lookout was still perched, keeping an eye to the horizon. The pirate had left no tracks in the watery wasteland. There was no telling where Scarfield and his crew were at this moment, although Daniel knew they must be near. It would be dark in a few hours. And the bloody butcher was out there, somewhere, watching and waiting.

CHAPTER EIGHT

⌐◦⌐

*T*HAT NIGHT, Mainwaring put on a double guard. He ordered the men who went below to sleep with their boots on and their weapons close at hand.

Of course, no one slept. Even the old hands lay awake in their hammocks, knowing at any moment they might be called to scramble onto the deck into a night filled with gunfire and explosions.

Daniel lay awake like the rest, trying not to think.

Just as the midnight bell was being struck, he fell asleep and had a vivid dream:

He saw himself from above, floating facedown in the ocean, like the dead bodies of the men he had seen that day. But before he could take in the full horror of the sight, the dream suddenly shifted and he was in his body, peering at the underwater world through his own eyes, hearing the sounds, muffled and indistinct, through his own ears. The water all around him glowed with a strange, milky-white light.

The waves foamed and surged around him, dragging him under. He tried to swim, but his arms and legs were numb from cold and exhaustion. As he sank, the thought flashed by that this was how his father must have felt in his last moments.

Above he could hear the curling and crashing of waves. Below there was a deep silence.

Then, all at once, a sword came tumbling through the water and fitted, as if by magic, into his hand. His fingers closed around the handle, and he felt sure and able.

He whipped the blade through the milky murk. To his astonishment, the white cloudy water parted before him. Overhead he could see blue sky, with white clouds drifting by. Holding fast to his sword, he broke through the surface, taking in a lungful of clean, pure air.

Daniel sat up in his hammock, his face glistening with sweat. He knew that death was there, in the darkness, waiting for him. For the first time since he had come onto the ship, he was truly afraid.

He wanted to call out for Killy. But he knew that was a foolish thought. He was ashamed of his fear.

So instead he reached down into the sea bag, which lay on the floor below him, and drew out his short sword. It was good to feel the firm leather grip beneath his fingers and the weathered roughness of the wooden scabbard that covered the blade.

As the images from the dream swirled about in his head, he settled back into his hammock, cradling the sword across his chest. In this way, he drifted off into a deep, dreamless sleep that lasted until dawn.

There was no attack that night. Or the next day. Or the next.

Daniel rose each morning and went about his work, mending and caulking the leaks in the hull, always with an eye on the horizon. Three days passed without any questionable sightings. Slowly the taut fear of the first few days relaxed into a state of vigilant attention.

Although Mainwaring cruised at a course designed to cross paths with the pirates, the ocean seemed deserted by the sea rovers. As Daniel understood it, the plan was to follow the coastline south, hoping to lure Scarfield into the open.

Mainwaring hailed every ship they passed. Calling through the speaking trumpet, he asked if the mariners had seen any pirate activity. In this way, he collected intelligence about Scarfield and his movements. Twice they ran across ships whose captains said they had not seen Scarfield but had heard that he was cruising the coastline.

One report, off the ragged coast of Virginia, told of Scarfield ambushing a sloop and plundering her before sending her and the crew to the watery depths. It seemed that the pirate was headed south, staying just ahead of Mainwaring and his crew, leaving rumors of smoking wreckage in his wake. Any day, they might catch him. Or be caught by him, as Killy pointed out. But for now, they would watch and wait.

Once the novelty wore off, Daniel found that life aboard ship followed a predictable pattern: He and Killy would rise early in the morning, stow their hammocks, and hang their sea bags from pegs on the wall in their quarters.

The crew was fed in the galley at tables swung from ropes overhead. They ate in shifts. Daniel soon learned the food aboard ship did nothing to rival Aunt Terra's cooking. Because the meat was preserved in barrels of brine, any resemblance to home cooking was soon snuffed out. The finest beef became a soggy, leathery mass of fibers which the old tars called salt junk.

Doctor Bones' main all-purpose dish was a stew made from brined pork, beef, or salt fish combined with dried potato slices—which resembled wood chips, and dried peas, which Daniel thought could just as easily have been used as musket balls.

Sometimes Bones would introduce some variety to the menu by adding a mush made from soaking the hardtack sea biscuits in water. Hardtack was simply flour and water, baked to rock-hard consistency in a flat iron skillet. Daniel often wondered whether they would be better off throwing the hardtack to the birds and eating the skillet instead.

For flavoring, each man was allowed a pound of butter and a half pint of vinegar a week. All of this culinary cruelty would have made a miserable impression on Daniel if it hadn't been for their daily ration of grog. Each man on ship was entitled to one gill of rum a day—about a cupful. And Daniel came to look forward to this daily offering like a child looks forward to Christmas.

As Killy said, "Grog's a drink what warms a man's innards without dulling his mind."

It was true. In all of the time he had been on the ship,

Daniel had never once seen anyone who looked or acted drunk.

After the morning meal, Daniel and Killy went about their tasks up on the deck or down in the hold, checking for leaks and repairing worn or broken spars. A few small leaks might have sprung in the hull, but they were easily able to repair by driving oakum into the cracks between the timbers with a hammer and a caulking chisel.

At noon came another of Dr. Bones' testaments to gastronomical absurdity, then they were back to work for the afternoon. The evening meal was served before dark and included their nightly ration of grog.

In the evening, Daniel and Killy would spend as much time as possible up on deck before going down into the stinking hold where they would perhaps take a sponge bath in cold water, then wrap themselves in their thin blankets, climb into their hammocks, and doze off to a restless, swaying sleep.

Officers stayed in their own world on the upper deck and in their cabins; enlisted men worked at their jobs and retired below decks in the evening. The gunnery crew did not mix with the marines, and the sailors did not pay the slightest attention to the carpenters.

It was a rigid society, with every task, every gesture and every verbal exchange governed by a bewildering set of rules and customs, which Daniel was only beginning to understand. In some ways, it was similar to the rough-handed world of the shipyard. But Daniel often felt as if he had wandered into a foreign country where the language and manners were strange and unsettling.

Many times, he wanted to go aloft to see the friendly face of the lookout. But the chance to climb did not come. And Daniel knew better than to ask to do something simply because he thought he would enjoy it.

Still, he was slowly becoming a part of the crew. His life at the shipyard and on the city streets seemed far away and very, very unimportant.

Early one morning off the coast of the Carolinas, as Daniel was standing at the rail dreaming about a long life at sea, he heard a call from the crow's nest:

"Ship to the northwest!"

The entire crew poured onto the deck and squinted across the sun-spangled water at a huge brigantine, which was bearing down on them at an incredible speed.

"She's a pirate, sure enough," Killy said, close to Daniel's ear. The boy felt his innards clench up tight.

"How do you know?" Daniel asked. They had not glimpsed a pirate craft until now.

The carpenter raised a hand to shade his eyes from the sun, "She's not flyin' a flag at all. And she's comin' up way too fast. She thinks we're a rich merchant prize, and by the way she's bearin' down on us, I'd say she thinks she can take us without a fight."

Daniel felt the blood pumping through his temples.

"Is it Scarfield?" he asked.

"We will know soon enough," Killy said. "She's closing on us fast! What was the name of Scarfield's ship?"

"The *Revenge*." Daniel breathed. "And I hear tell she has red sails!"

"Battle stations!" Mr. Buckthorn called out.

Men began to scramble about like bees in a hive. The armorer frantically handed out weapons and ammunition. The gunners rolled back their cannons and propped open the gun ports. Sailors sprang to the rigging, ready for the captain's orders. The marines took up their sharpshooting positions on the upper deck.

Daniel and Killy got their water buckets and set them handy by the gunners' positions. On the upper deck, Daniel could see Mainwaring, standing by Mr. Buckthorn at the wheel. His right hand rested on the hilt of the long sword at his belt.

Daniel checked his own weapons. His pistol was primed, loaded, and ready to fire. His short sword dangled at his belt, where he could get it quickly.

The dark ship had appeared so suddenly that Daniel had no time to be afraid. But now, as it plowed toward them, Daniel noticed that his legs had begun to tremble so badly that he had to brace himself against the wall to keep on his feet.

Mainwaring gave orders to turn the *Sea Turtle* broadside. The gunnery mate ordered his men to load their guns and prepare to fire.

But before the mysterious ship came within cannon range, she cut her sails and slipped off to the east. Now the full sun was behind her, and Daniel had to shield his eyes with his hand to see anything.

"What are they doing?" he asked Killy.

The carpenter was checking his pistol.

"An old trick. Now the sun is in our eyes. I think they mean to board us, lad."

Daniel swallowed. This was the battle he had dreaded— and anticipated—for so long.

"Don't be forgettin' what I said," Killy growled. "If the devils should force their way onto our decks, it will be every man for himself. Use your pistol and sword. Don't be afraid to blow the brains out of any sea devil who tries to lay a hand on you."

"I won't," Daniel said. But he was trembling so badly that he wondered if he could defend himself.

"Will they send a boarding party?" Daniel asked.

Killy shook his head.

"I don't know. They may rake us with cannon fire first. But, I will tell you this—Wait! For the love of God, look at that!"

In the glaring light, Daniel could see a black flag being hauled to the topmast of the approaching ship. When the wind caught it, he could clearly make out the crossed bones and the white death-skull of the sea robbers. No, he had to admit, their sails were not red. They were pale, pale as moonlight.

At that instant, a bloodcurdling howl went up from the deck of the dark ship, carrying clear across the water. Daniel's heart almost failed him. How many men were crammed onto the deck of the ship? One hundred and fifty, perhaps two hundred? It was impossible to tell.

Squinting hard into the sun, Daniel could see that the frigate was a mere hundred yards away. The pirates were lowering their longboats.

Daniel felt his bowels turn to liquid. He watched, with strange fascination, as heavily armed men scrambled down the rope lines and dropped into the boats like rats. As soon as the pitching crafts were full, the rowers set their oars and came for the *Sea Turtle*. With alarming speed, they were closing in, six boats, crammed to the gills with howling men.

"You will fire on my command," the gunner's mate thundered, "not before. Then you will reload like the devil himself and rake them again. I will have the hide of any man who shirks his duty. Hold fast, men!"

Now Daniel caught sight of the lead boat. It was coming along fast. He shielded his eyes from the sunlight with his hand and looked down.

Men of every race and color, dressed in outlandish garb, were pulling on the oars, shoulder to shoulder. Each one was armed with a forest of weapons: Their chests were crossed with broad sashes that held six or eight deadly pistols. Their boots and bandoliers and belts bristled with cutting edges: axes and swords and daggers.

When the boat was less than fifty yards away, one of the men rose and climbed forward, balancing himself precariously at the bow.

He was dressed in a wild assortment of ragged clothing, including an ornate coat whose tails flapped in the wind. The sleeves had been torn away, and his hairy arms were blue with tattoos. His torso was festooned with a broad sash that carried a deadly array of pistols and cutlery. His hair and long beard stuck out in every direction, like the branches of a twisted tree.

Close at hand, Daniel heard the gunnery mate shout: "Fire your piece!"

An instant later, the air was filled with the deep-throated boom of the cannons and the stench of sulfurous smoke. Daniel choked and ducked down by the gun port, trying to catch his breath.

Looking around, he saw that the water before them was obscured by a thick cloud. But when the breeze swept the cloud away, he saw the armada of longboats capsized and splintered. All around the sinking wreckage, men with bloody heads and ragged arms paddled desperately in the lifting ocean.

Back on the deck of the pirate craft, the gunnery crew was ready. They opened up with a full barrage, splitting the salty air with the thunderclap of their cannons, filling the sky with deadly balls. Daniel crouched low and heard the shots hurtle through the rigging overhead. They were aiming high.

With astonishing speed, the pirates reloaded and raked them again and again, lowering their aim and pounding the body of the *Sea Turtle* until the deck trembled under their feet. Then, as suddenly as it had begun, the barrage ended.

"Now their blood is up," he heard Killy shout.

But this was only the beginning.

When the smoke began to clear, Daniel could see many boats lowered from the dark craft. Men poured into them and began to stroke for the *Sea Turtle*.

Then Daniel saw that the lead boat had somehow survived the barrage of cannon fire. The boat was within musket range now, and Daniel could hear the sharp crack of the marines' shoulder arms. Bullets pelted the water all around the marauders' boat.

As the bullets whizzed around him, the cursing pirate made no attempt to shield himself. Instead he exposed himself even more by rising onto the bow and drawing two pistols from his bandolier.

Then, when they were less than thirty yards from the ship, he did something even more astonishing. Howling like a banshee, he pointed the barrels of his pistols at the boards beneath his feet and pulled both triggers, blowing a huge hole in the bow.

The boat began to sink. Pulling desperately for their lives, the pirate crew worked the oars like madmen. A hailstorm of bullets rained down around them.

But the pirate had accomplished his purpose. He was in under the muzzles of the cannons now. And he knew his men had no choice but to make for the *Sea Turtle* and scale her sides.

The longboat was half filled with water when it reached the sides of the ship. One of the pirates tossed a grappling hook up and snared a gun port. Before anyone could cut it away, three of the sinewy intruders were up the rope, over the gunwale, and leaping in among the crew of the number-nine gun, hacking the men to pieces with their broadswords.

A dozen marines flung themselves at the attackers,

swinging their swords. The clang of steel rang like bells. The marines fought well. But they were buried by a waterfall of pirates that poured over the side of the ship and onto the deck. Quickly the situation became very serious. The marines, Mainwaring's best fighting men, were cut down and left to die.

Daniel watched all of this with a horrible fascination. Then he turned and saw something even more frightening.

Many more men, cutlasses and pistols clutched in their hands, were swarming over every side of the ship and dropping onto the deck. They were coming from all directions, and Daniel grasped, in a moment of terrible clarity, that the *Sea Turtle* was entirely surrounded.

The pirates began lighting and tossing hand bombs into the confused ranks of Mainwaring's men. When these explosive balls went off, with dull thuds and sudden flashes of blinding light, men lost their arms and legs. Some were ripped open from throat to belly and staggered around on the deck.

Daniel looked up just in time to see a wild-eyed pirate coming toward him, a pistol in each hand. Daniel raised his piece and fired. As soon as he pulled the trigger, he knew it was a bad shot. The ball went high and wild and thudded into the wooden mast ten feet above the pirate's head. The buccaneer never even looked at him. He just ducked into the battle smoke and began breaking skulls with his handguns.

Daniel knelt and began to reload, instantly regretting that he had only one pistol. He knew he was helpless, crouched on the deck with an empty gun.

A man fell beside him, splattering blood across Daniel's face and hands. When Daniel turned to look, he could see that the sailor's head was missing. All that remained was a blackened, smoking stump.

Daniel tried to reload his firearm, but his hands were trembling so badly that he could not. In his clumsiness, he dropped his ramrod. The iron bar rolled off across the deck and disappeared in the clouds of cannon smoke. He went down on his hands and knees and crawled on the deck, groping for the ramrod.

Someone trampled on his hand with a heavy boot. Daniel dropped his pistol and painfully worked his fingers. Good. Nothing was broken.

Cradling his throbbing hand, he crawled back against the wall of the ship.

The cannons thundered, and the grunts and curses of the fighting men grew louder, melding into a roar that made Daniel's ears ache. The smoke from the cannons and the small-arms fire grew so thick that he could scarcely breathe.

Taking in one sulfurous breath after another, Daniel closed his tearing eyes and wedged himself back into a small space between two water barrels. He drew his legs up to his chest and bowed his head, with his eyes clamped shut.

He had no way of knowing how long he stayed hidden between the water barrels. All he knew was that he was suddenly aware of a strange quiet. His ears still ringing, Daniel lifted his head and looked around.

Men—some hacked beyond recognition, some groping and moaning—littered the deck. Some, half-buried in a debris of severed rigging and splinters, crawled about like stunned animals. Everywhere men were rising like ghosts, shaking themselves, and slapping the dust from their clothing. It was a strange sight.

Daniel sat and stared, openmouthed, as if watching a painting come to life. It was only after he had gawked at this spectacle for a few heartbeats that he realized the men who moved about were not pirates, but the crew of the *Sea Turtle*. Most of the men who lay slumped on the deck were the pirates. There were a few marines and sailors lying still, but very few.

Daniel pulled himself to his feet. He saw that the pirate ship was gone. All around the *Sea Turtle*, the shattered remains of the longboats tossed about in a colorful, floating mass of wreckage.

Just then, Killy came toward him through the smoke.

"Dan, there you are!"

"Did we win?" Daniel asked, his throat raw and parched. Killy laughed.

"Aye, lad, we won. It was touch and go there for a while. Looks like you came through all right. Did you use your sword like I told you?"

"No," Daniel said lamely. "I used my pistol mostly."

A dark stain of shame crept through him. Even though he didn't think anyone knew what he had done, he knew. He had emerged from his first battle as a miserable coward.

But before he could dwell on his own misery, Killy shook him by the shoulders. "Dan," he said urgently, "you told me you could swim, is that right?"

Daniel nodded. That was not a lie. He could swim, and swim well.

"Good," Killy said, taking him by the elbow and leading him across the deck. "We need you to do some swimming for us now. One of the sea devils' cannonballs punched a hole in our ship the size of a watermelon. Water is pourin' in faster than we can pump it out.

"Unless we can get that hole plugged, we'll sink within the hour. I've tried to plug it from the inside but it's no good, the water's just coming in too fast. So we've gotta use an old sea carpenter's trick: We've doubled a large square of canvas and tied a long rope to each corner. Two of the ropes will be fastened to rigging on this side.

"You and I will leap overboard. Each of us will have the lead end of one of the remaining ropes tied 'round our waists. We've got to swim entirely under the hull of the ship and come up on the other side. Some of the tars will be waitin' for us there with a boat. They'll take the ropes from us and pull that patch up into place, coverin' the hole. The canvas will swell in the water and make a tight seal, temporary at best, but it will slow the leakin' enough for us to pump the water out of our hold and patch the hole. You understand what we're about to do, then?"

Daniel was instantly alert. He nodded and began to pull off his boots.

"Keep your feet covered," Killy warned him. "The underside of the hull is covered with razor-sharp barnacles; they'll tear you to pieces if you scrape up against them."

Daniel nodded. Before he had time to think, he had tied the rope across his chest, climbed up onto the sidewall, taken a deep breath, and jumped feetfirst into the cold water. He sank like a rock, down into the gray-white chill of the ocean. For a moment, the strange dream that had terrified him a few nights before flitted through his mind.

But Daniel knew this was no time for dreaming. Swimming with powerful strokes, he angled down along the dark hull, being careful to stay clear of the barnacles that glinted, green and sharp-edged, in the dim light. Off to his right, he caught a glimpse of Killy, diving deep with his own rope. Then he saw the gaping hole. It was surprisingly low, a good ten feet below the waterline, almost through the keel. A swirl of water corkscrewed through the splintered opening, rushing into the hold.

As he swam past the damage, he saw the canvas settling down over the puncture, just as Killy said it would. He lingered a moment, to make sure the patch was fitted properly. He saw that Killy was already below him, diving deep under the keel, pulling his rope taught against the damaged hull. A good fit!

Daniel turned and dove, following his partner into the depths.

As he did, he felt a sharp tug from behind. Glancing back, he saw that his rope had snagged against the hull, forming a loop. His right ankle was tangled in the rope. As he was turning to free himself, a milky-white cloud settled around him. He tried to swim his way out of it. But it quickly surrounded him.

Frantically, Daniel twisted and turned. But it settled against him, closing him in. Then he realized what had happened: He had swum up into the canvas. If the sailcloth had not been doubled, he could have swum out of it easily. But it was doubled, forming a kind of envelope—an envelope that he was now trapped inside.

He pawed his way along the watery fabric, but he couldn't find the edge. The heavy material began to settle around him like a death shroud. Daniel knew he was running desperately short of air, and he was keenly aware that he might die this way, trapped inside the sailcloth.

Suddenly he was slammed up against the solid surface of the hull and felt the rope pulled tight, trapping him there. He could feel the sharp barnacles pressing through the canvas. His air was very low now. He knew that he had only a few seconds to save himself. Killy was nowhere in sight.

The images from the dream the night before flashed through his mind. There he was, going down in the murky water. Then he remembered his sword. He reached down and was overjoyed to find that it still hung faithfully at his belt. With a great effort, he drew the blade and thrusted out at the milky-white fabric, just as he had in his dream.

The blade tore through the canvas, making a short slit along the edge, just big enough for him to get his sword arm through. He forced his head through the hole and could see light pouring down from above.

A moment more and he had freed his other arm, then his

torso, and finally, wiggling like a fish, his legs and feet. Then, just as he had in the dream, he held firmly to his sword. He dove under the keel and came up on the far side, stroking hard for the surface, his lungs burning. Then, he broke the surface alongside the longboat and a dozen hands were hauling him into the boat and wrestling the coil of rope from his waist. Daniel lay on his back, staring at the sky, still clutching his sword.

He was alive!

What was more, the sailors were all around him, clapping him on the shoulder and smiling.

Killy was in the boat as well, soaked and gasping for air.

"We did it, lad!" the old carpenter shouted hoarsely. "The patch held!"

Too weak to answer, Daniel collapsed like a cloth doll as he was passed from one strong set of arms to another, all the way up onto the deck.

Daniel lay on his back on the deck, still gasping for air. It was good to feel the solid planks beneath him. It was good to be out in the sunlight, far above the dark and watery world that had almost taken his life.

Then he saw Mainwaring, standing nearby, with his hands on his hips and a faint smile on his face.

The captain didn't say anything, but Daniel could tell by the look in his eye that he was pleased.

When Daniel caught his breath, he slipped his sword into its scabbard and sat up. Something jabbed him, under his right leg. He reached down and picked it up. Daniel grinned.

It was his ramrod.

CHAPTER NINE

$\mathcal{D}$ANIEL WAS SHOCKED by the sheer destruction of the battle.

During the fight, dozens of cannonballs had been lobbed at the *Sea Turtle*. Some, like the one that had punched through the hull, had done serious damage. Others flew high or wide and only splintered the wood or ripped through sailcloth and rigging.

Daniel learned that the pirates had also stuffed the barrels of their cannons with chains, iron bars, and bags of nails. The deadly evidence of these "junk shots" was still embedded in the timbers and hull of the ship.

He was amazed to learn that the entire encounter, from the first sighting of the ship to its mysterious departure, had lasted less than an hour. Once the pirates saw they were defeated, they cut their losses and ran, leaving behind their dead and dying.

It took the crew two days to put the ship back into order. Killy and Daniel worked from dawn to dusk patching holes and repairing the splintered and broken spars. The deadly gash in the hull required an elaborate wooden plug, pitched and caulked and hammered into place. It took hours to pump the bilge water from the hold.

The seamen scrubbed the deck with a slurry of loose sand. But try as they might, they couldn't erase the bloodstains. It was as if the dying pirates had etched a tattoo onto the deck, as a permanent souvenir of the fight.

But the pirates were not the only ones who had bled. Many of Mainwaring's men had suffered wounds. Hardly anyone had come through the battle without, at the very least, some bruise or scrape.

Some men paid more dearly. A final count showed that twelve of the *Sea Turtle's* crew had died in the brief fight. Six marines, four seamen, and two gunners lay dead. Mainwaring ordered a formal burial at sea, with the entire crew up on deck to pay their respects.

As the dead were lifted and lowered over the side, Daniel wanted to look away. But something also made him take in the full horror of it. As he was running his eyes over the pale faces, Daniel stopped and caught his breath. He recognized one of them. He was the young marksman who, just a few days before, had been showing him how to load and shoot a pistol. Daniel had never even learned the man's name, and now he was sliding into the water, food for the fish.

Daniel stared at the patch of metallic-blue ocean that marked the young man's watery grave. For the first time, he began to grapple with the very real possibility that he could be dead in the next hour, sent to the ocean floor, just like the young marine.

Daniel glanced at Killy and the other men who clustered around him. They stood, just as he did, watching the bodies slipping into the sea.

Daniel wondered how these men could go into battle knowing their lives were held only by the fragile threads of chance. But he knew the answer: They didn't think about it. If they did, he realized, they would go mad.

So Daniel did what men in combat have always done. He made a conscious decision to close down the part of the brain where scary thoughts dwell, and he went about his job, attending to the task at hand.

The pirates' hacked and gunshot bodies had been dumped unceremoniously over the side just after the battle, so it was difficult to get an accurate count of the dead. But the best estimates were that between twenty and thirty of the sea rovers had been cut down in the fight. Daniel heard that the wild-haired pirate chieftain had been among the last to die and had staggered around the deck, discharging his pistols until he could no longer stand.

They never learned the name of the pirate captain or what had happened to the remains of his ragged crew. All they knew was that whoever had been left aboard the pirate ship had vanished in the distance, in search of easier prey.

Mainwaring sailed south, instructing his men to keep an eye on the horizon and a hand on their weapons.

In the next ten days, the crew racked up an astonishing series of victories. They employed a simple tactic: As planned, they posed as a merchant ship, they lured the sea wolves within cannon range, then rolled out the guns and blew them apart before the pirates recognized their mistake.

With surprise on their side, Mainwaring's crew also

captured and burned seven pirate ships. They were small boats—mostly schooners encrusted with barnacles and embedded with junk shot. These miserable craft were filled with ragged, drunken men who were no match for the crew of the *Sea Turtle*.

The ships burned like paper and sank without a trace.

A few of the craftier pirate chieftains got away—pulling back when they realized they were losing and retreating over the horizon. Word of the *Sea Turtle*'s ferociousness spread through the pirate world, from one landfall to the next, until Mainwaring's name caused a stir whenever it was mentioned.

But James Mainwaring was not satisfied. Despite his many victories, his biggest prize still eluded him: Captain Scarfield remained a terrifying mystery.

Off the coast of Florida, they had come within an hour of running Scarfield down. But they arrived too late, finding only the smoking hulk of a ship and a few survivors floating in a lifeboat, tales of Scarfield's cruelty on their lips.

It seemed that the pirate captain was mocking them, allowing them within striking range, then slipping away. The fact remained that after three weeks of relentless searching, the crew of the *Sea Turtle* had not even spotted Scarfield's vessel from a distance.

One evening, Mainwaring called Daniel to his quarters. It was the first time they had spoken privately during the entire voyage.

"Come in," Mainwaring said when the boy knocked at his cabin door.

The captain was seated at his dining table, which was bolted to the floor in the center of the room. He looked tired and, Daniel thought, older.

"Are you being treated well?" Mainwaring asked.

"Yes, sir."

Mainwaring smiled.

"I have a few questions for you," he said.

"Of course, sir."

"How much do you know about the Caribbean ports? Perhaps your uncle talked in some detail about the islands?"

Daniel thought for a moment.

"I can't say anything for sure, sir. I mean, he talked in a general way. But he never said anything to me about the specifics of his voyages."

Mainwaring looked disappointed.

"I see. Did he ever mention criminal activity in that region?"

"No, sir."

Mainwaring sighed.

He unrolled a nautical chart on a tabletop and weighted the ends down with books. He began speaking, as much to himself as to Daniel.

"We have traced our way down the coastline and have very nearly reached the tip of Florida. We are approaching the point of no return. I must decide to return to Philadelphia empty-handed or push on into the Caribbean—into the pirate's own hunting grounds.

"Time is running out. In a few weeks, the summer will be over, and Scarfield will surely be in the Caribbean, where he can hide out for the winter on any one of a thousand tiny islands or secret coves, without any fear of being discovered. If I can stay on his trail, we may be able to run him down before he disappears into his nest. One of the merchant captains told me that Scarfield is rumored to have a hideout on Hispaniola."

"Hispaniola?" Daniel said.

"You've heard of it?"

"Only the name. Where is it?"

Mainwaring jabbed his finger at the chart. "Here. We can be there in two days. I must decide quickly."

Daniel swallowed.

"It is a bold plan," he ventured.

"Is this your way of saying that it is a foolish plan?"

"Many things could go wrong."

"Aye, but Scarfield will not expect us to follow him into his own waters. Once we cross into the tropics, we will be totally on our own, outmanned and outgunned, sailing into a region where there is no law and no hope for rescue if we should fail.

"But we will have surprise on our side. I expect that once he leaves the Floridian waters, Scarfield will drop his guard. And once he relaxes, we will rush upon him like a hurricane."

Daniel stared down at the outlines of the island.

"It could work," he said, not sure if his opinion counted for anything.

Mainwaring smiled.

"It surely could," he said.

The Captain offered his hand.

"You have a good head on your shoulders," he said. "And a good ear. Sometimes a man just needs to hear himself talk to arrive at a decision. I have made up my mind."

"Yes, sir?"

Mainwaring laughed.

"We are sailing south!"

The officer opened the door and called, "Mister Buckthorn! If you please, sir, we have a course to chart!"

Daniel nodded and left, making his way up onto the deck, not sure if he should feel terrified or excited. He had wanted adventure, sure enough. And now he was in the midst of it.

The next morning, when Mr. Buckthorn announced Mainwaring's decision to the crew, they roared. But later, below deck, Daniel heard some of the old hands talking in hushed tones about the foolhardiness of sailing straight into a harbor where every other ship was a pirate vessel and where every man, woman, and child on the island had some connection to the pirate trade.

Daniel asked Killy about the island. The carpenter shook his head.

"I never been there," he admitted, "but there's many a man aboard who has. Let's talk to Charley Boatknife. I know he's been ashore and escaped to tell the tale."

They were soon settled up on the deck of the ship, where Charley sat smoking a fragrant bulldog pipe. Daniel had not spoken with him since the day of his perilous climb to the crow's nest. But the old mariner remembered him well enough.

"I haven't been there in years," Charley began, "but if what the others tell me is true, the place is still as dangerous and harrowing a landfall as the Creator ever turned his back on. It's the Devil's island, sure enough, and no man, lest he is in league with the Devil, should venture there."

"What's it like?" Daniel asked, wide-eyed.

"It's a large and rich island, located at seventeen to nineteen degrees latitude, deep in the tropics, just a shade above the equator. This was the island Christopher Columbus discovered in fourteen-ninety-two. The Spaniards have had possession of it ever since. And a wild and uncivilized place it is—black, Indian, and white races all mixed together and tossed about.

"The isle's got one large city called Santo Domingo, surrounded by rich plantations, meadows, and fruitful gardens. Many a wily pirate captain has retired there and lived out his days like a king. Thousands of black slaves, captured and brought from the interior of Africa, arrive by boat and are put to work in the fields. They grow ginger and tobacco, oranges and lemons, as well as the world's richest cocoa. The countryside is overflowing with beasts, both wild and tame. I once hunted wild boar there. The fishing is excellent, and the giant sea tortoises are a delicacy that can be found nowhere else in the world.

"It's an island of fine rivers and good seaports. You'd think it would be a Garden of Eden. But it is actually a pit of depravity. The governors are in league with the pirates, and each city is a steaming morass of grog-shops and dance halls. The streets themselves are the scenes of every imaginable act of lewd and drunken behavior the human mind can conjure up.

"And speaking of conjuring—the native people there are great healers and sorcerers and can cure or kill a man with their magic.

"One thing is for sure: When you go to Hispaniola, you leave behind the orderliness of the known world. You enter the tropics, where everything you know is turned upside down."

Daniel lay in his hammock that night and turned Charley's words over in his mind. What was he to think? He had sworn off thinking. All he knew was that in a very short time, he would be in Hispaniola and he would see for himself.

CHAPTER TEN

⌐~∞~⌐

*J*UST AS MAINWARING had predicted, in two day's time, they reached Hispaniola.

Even from a distance, Daniel could smell the vegetation. The heavy, languid, rum-and-molasses scent of tropical fruits and flowers floated like exotic perfume across the water and into his land-hungry nostrils.

Then the isle itself came into view: A lush jewel of greenery set in the emerald blue of the ocean. The white sandy beaches were fringed with palm trees, and the Spanish buildings, with their towering steeples and rounded domes, were surrounded by gardens. This was the fabled city of Santo Domingo.

But as the ship came closer and slipped into the turquoise waters of the harbor, Daniel could see the other, darker aspects of the island paradise: The waterway was clogged with a mass of anchored ships of every size and description. Many were bristling with cannons and openly flew the black flag of the Brethren of the Coast. Colorfully dressed men went about their tasks on the boats, shouting to one another.

On the docks, Daniel could see the men who worked in

the hot sun, straining as they handled barrels and boxes and packages. Beyond the docks, huge dusty streets led back into the heart of the city.

"Battle stations!" Mr. Buckthorn sang out.

But he didn't need to give the order. Every man was already in his place. Everyone knew that the events of the next hour would decide whether Mainwaring was a brilliant tactical genius or an overconfident fool.

Daniel kept an eye on the captain as he stood on the upper deck, with Mr. Buckthorn at the wheel. Mainwaring was surveying the anchored ships with a long spyglass. He seemed to be paying special attention to a well-rigged schooner that was anchored offshore, away from the rest of the boats. It was, perhaps, fifty-feet long and sat low in the water.

Daniel was surprised to see Mr. Hibbington approaching him.

"Captain wants to see you," the boatswain said.

"What's this all about?" Killy asked.

Hibbington ignored the carpenter's remark and nodded his head in the captain's direction.

"You best come along," was all he would say.

Daniel shrugged at Killy and followed Hibbington across the deck, climbing the stairs to the captain's position.

"Yes, sir?" Daniel asked.

Mainwaring's usual jaunty smile was gone, replaced by a puzzled frown.

"Have a look at that schooner," the commander said. He

handed Daniel the spyglass.

The boy set his eye to the glass and peered across the water. He could scarcely believe his eyes.

"Uncle Elias' ship." Daniel whispered, more to himself than to Mainwaring.

Then he set his eye to the glass again, just to make sure he wasn't making some foolish mistake. Sure enough, it was the *Good Samaritan*. And there, on the upper deck, dressed in his peaceful Quaker's coat and wearing his somber black hat, was the unmistakable outline of Captain Collins, raising his own spyglass.

Daniel ducked out of sight, handing the glass back to Mainwaring.

"What's he doing in these waters?" the captain asked.

"I don't know," Daniel answered honestly.

Mainwaring frowned.

"Go to the compartment in my cabin and hide yourself," he ordered.

"Yes, sir."

"And don't come out until I send for you."

"No, sir. Of course not."

Daniel turned and headed for the cabin. He knew that if his uncle spotted him, he would have a lot of explaining to do. And he surely wanted to avoid that. But his curiosity was so great he couldn't resist lingering by the cabin door to see what would happen next.

They drifted to within a hundred yards of the schooner. Then, with a nod to Mr. Hibbington, Mainwaring snatched up his speaking trumpet.

"Avast, Captain Collins!" he called. His words carried sure and strong across the water.

No answer.

"I say again, Captain Collins. Greetings from an old friend!"

There was a long pause.

Then Collins answered, speaking through his own trumpet: "James Mainwaring! What a pleasure! May I have permission to come aboard?"

Mainwaring nodded, and answered, "Come along as you please."

Daniel saw the crew of the *Good Samaritan* lower a small boat. His uncle and four oarsmen climbed down and pushed off. Daniel sank back into the shadows.

When the boat was secured, Captain Collins and his men climbed aboard the *Sea Turtle*.

"Friend James," the Quaker exclaimed, "how fine to see thee in these waters!"

They shook hands warmly.

"Come to my cabin where we can visit in comfort," he heard Mainwaring say.

Daniel rushed into Mainwaring's cabin, knocking over a pile of maps. But there was no time to pick them up. He slipped behind the louvered closet door and pulled it closed, then crouched in the darkness, breathing rapidly.

He heard them come into the cabin. He closed his eyes and tried to still himself, knowing that he must not move or shift on the creaking floorboards, and that Uncle Elias was seated not six feet from where he hid.

Squinting through the slats, Daniel saw Mainwaring produce a bottle of Jamaican rum and fill two glasses, handing one to Collins.

"Now," the older man said brightly, "if we had our chessboard, we could play a fine game, just like we used to back on Spruce Street."

Mainwaring smiled. "Well, the officers and I do play now and then. Shall we play a game, for old-time's sake?"

Before Daniel could do anything about it, Mainwaring walked to the closet, opened the door a few inches and reached over Daniel's shoulder, taking the wooden box of chess pieces from a shelf just over his head.

Daniel's face was beaded with sweat. Mainwaring seemed relaxed, confident. And why shouldn't he be? Collins sat comfortably in his chair, smiling pleasantly as he sipped his rum. He had seen nothing.

Then the door was closed and Daniel set his eyes to the slats once again. He watched as they set the chessboard out on the table.

"Tell me," he heard Mainwaring say, "how is dear Terra? And your niece . . . I'm sorry . . . I've forgotten her name?"

"Hettie."

"Yes, dear Hettie. And the boy, Daniel, how is he?"

"All were well when I left," Collins said.

The Quaker began his game by advancing a pawn.

"I must confess," Collins said, "that while I am away on these voyages, I do have some apprehension about Hettie."

Mainwaring moved one of his own pawns forward.

"Why is that?" he asked.

"I have the oddest sensation that she is being courted by some stranger, someone who wishes to remain secret. A mystery man, thee might say. I have made it very clear to her that she must choose someone who is of the proper station in Quaker society. Tell me, has she ever mentioned anything of this sort to thee?"

Mainwaring answered. "No, absolutely not. I know she has many admirers. But she never gave me any indication that she had given her heart to any of them."

Collins nodded, staring down at the board.

"Forgive me for asking," he said. "I just thought that she might have confided something to thee. Young people often do that amongst themselves, when the older folk are not listening."

Mainwaring glanced down at the board, unable to meet Collins' gaze directly.

Collins advanced his bishop. Several more plays went forward in silence. The center of the board quickly filled with pieces as each player sought to find some advantage over the other.

At last, Collins broke the silence. "I have heard rumors," he said slowly, "that thy campaign to rid the Atlantic coast of pirates has been eminently successful."

Now that the topic of conversation had shifted, Mainwaring forged ahead with his own questions. He moved his knight into play, leaping over a row of pawns.

"Yes," he said. "So successful, in fact, that I have even ventured into these waters, trying to hunt the pirates out on their own grounds. That is why I am here. But I must confess, I am curious to know why you are here. A merchant such as yourself is in constant danger among these cut-throats. What business could be so urgent that you would expose yourself to such danger?"

Collins smiled, "James, I will let thee in on a secret: I learned long ago that the shipping business works on one simple principle: The greater the risk, the greater the reward. I go where no other traders will. This way, I can secure the greatest prices for my goods."

Mainwaring lifted his head. "Captain Collins, I must ask you, with all due respect, to be frank with me. I suspect that you are not telling me everything, and there is some hidden reason why you sail these waters. Please reveal it to me now, or I will be forced to send my marines over to search your ship."

The Quaker smiled. "Thee have no legal jurisdiction in this region," he said.

"I do not need any," Mainwaring asserted. "This is an unofficial mission. I am a bounty hunter. My only responsibility is to my investors."

At this, Captain Collins set down his glass. The lines around his mouth tightened, then relaxed into a warm grin. "Since thee have asked," Collins said, "I will tell thee as plainly as I can: It is precisely because of the pirates that I am in these waters."

Daniel felt a tingle ripple down his spine. He leaned closer to the slits in the door.

"I learned long ago," Captain Collins said, "that pirates are only men. And as men, they must eat. But who will sell them their flour and cornmeal? I will. For a price ten times what the same cargo would fetch in the colonies."

Collins saw the dismayed look on Mainwaring's face and gave a short laugh.

"Oh, don't look so shocked . . . The pirates are good customers. At least, they pay their bills, which is more than I can say for many. And I have no hand in their bloody deeds. It is simply a matter of selling on my part and buying on theirs."

"So," Mainwaring said slowly, "this is how you have amassed your wealth: by dealing with pirates, while you pretend to lead a moral life among your Quaker associates in Philadelphia. That, sir, is despicable."

Captain Collins sighed.

"Thy words are true," he said sadly. "I admit, I have betrayed my own conscience. But everyone must make compromises. Remember, Friend James, poverty itself is a compromise. Besides, most men keep secrets from one another. Why, for all I know, there is some great secret that thee are keeping from me.

"Come now, Friend James, is there anything thee wish to tell me? Unburden thyself, it is good for the soul."

Mainwaring straightened his back. "Yes, I do have a secret. And I am tiring of this game you play with me. I don't mind telling you that I love Hettie and plan to marry her, with or without your consent."

Collins listened impassively. Then he leaned forward.

"Well," he said, "this places each of us in a very awkward situation, does it not?"

"I would say I have the upper hand," Mainwaring said.

"How is that?"

"I have a very able crew. I could board your ship now and seize everything you have as contraband."

Collins smiled. He reached down and picked up his queen, moving her forward into the field of battle. He sat back in his chair and surveyed Mainwaring coolly. "Maybe," he said at last, "maybe thee would not be such a bad husband for Hettie after all."

"I would be a fine husband for Hettie," Mainwaring declared. "In fact, if all goes well, I should be prepared to marry your niece within the month. Once I have captured Scarfield—"

"Oh," Collins said, "so it's Scarfield thee art after?"

"Well, of course. I thought you knew that."

Collins smiled again. "Well, I thought thee had given up on him. I mean, thee hast been victorious over so many other pirate crews. What is it about Scarfield that interests thee so?"

"He is the one I was sent to hunt down. Until I have him, my mission is incomplete."

"Well, perhaps I can help thee."

"Do you know of his whereabouts?" Mainwaring asked.

"Of course," Collins said casually. "He is one of my best customers. Why, Captain Scarfield and I sat in the cabin of the *Good Samaritan* just a few hours ago, drinking Jamaican rum and talking wheat prices.

Mainwaring's face reddened. "That devil was on your ship?"

"Of course."

"Where is he now?"

"I have no idea."

"Don't toy with me."

"I am speaking the truth. Pirates do not reveal their hiding places, even to trusted business associates. Why, there are hundreds of nearby coves and islands where he could conceal himself."

"But you can send word to him?"

"Of course. A few words dropped at the right tavern and a signal of fluttering flags are all that is needed to bring him running."

"All right, Captain," Mainwaring replied. "I will strike a bargain with you, an unholy bargain, but a bargain all the same. If you will help me capture Scarfield and will not interfere with my marriage to Hettie, I will give you your freedom and will not reveal the truth back in Philadelphia, about your so-called shipping business. Is this agreeable?"

Collins glanced down at the chessboard, seeming to look for an escape.

"Very well," he said at last.

"All right then," Mainwaring said. "We will set a trap. You and your men shall be the bait. You will arrange for Scarfield to meet you aboard your ship. I will be waiting below your decks with my marines. We will take them by surprise, without harming you or your precious crew. Once I have possession of Scarfield and his ship, you will be free to go. We will not speak of this again."

Collins nodded. "I will agree so long as thee can assure

the safety of myself and my crew. I have no wish to become involved in bloodshed."

Mainwaring sneered. "You are involved, you old liar. You have waded up to your neck in blood. And only God in Heaven can decide how you shall pay. But I'll look to your safety, be assured of that."

"Thy word is good enough for me," Collins said.

The men were quiet now, for an unusually long time. At last, the Quaker stood and said, "I must go and make preparations," he said. "Perhaps we can finish our game later." Then he put on his hat. Daniel listened as his uncle and Mainwaring climbed the stairs to the deck and vanished.

In a few minutes, Mainwaring was back. "Come out," the officer ordered.

Daniel pushed the door aside and stepped into the room. Even in the poor light, he could see that Mainwaring's face was flushed with anger.

"If there is one thing I hate," the captain said testily, "it is a hypocrite."

Daniel nodded. He could not disagree. His mind raced backward in time. Suddenly everything he had thought and felt about his uncle, his family, and his sheltered life was turned upside down. Every conversation that had taken place in the house on Spruce Street had to be seen in a new light. And every one of his uncle's long absences now took on a darker, more sinister meaning.

"Imagine—" Mainwaring was still seething. "All these years, that conniver has played the perfect Quaker, so pious and humble, looking down his nose at the bounty hunter and the military man! And all the while, he was lining his pockets with pirate gold!"

Daniel nodded.

"It's hard to believe," he said. "I should have known—or suspected."

Mainwaring shook his head. "Don't blame yourself, boy. He certainly had me fooled. I've dealt with many a shady character. But I never noticed the stink of impropriety on him."

"What should we do now?" Daniel asked.

"I'll tell you this much," Mainwaring said, "we can't let the old liar see you here. That would complicate things immeasurably. You keep yourself hidden."

"Yes, sir."

From that moment forward, Daniel was never far from his hiding place.

That night, he sat at the table in Mainwaring's cabin, picking at a plate of salt beef and trying to sort through a riot of thoughts. He felt a terrible rage against his uncle. To be betrayed in this way, by a man he had trusted and admired—that was a crushing blow. And to think he had felt jealous of Mainwaring. At least, this military man was honest about his desires. At least, he did not hide his true self under a humble Quaker coat.

Daniel sighed. The past was a hopeless tangle. And the future was pressing hard against him, demanding he stay awake and alert.

He turned his attention to his weapons. His pistol was

primed and stuck into his belt. His sword was stowed in the closet, where he could get it quickly. These things were solid and reliable. They did not change. They were not like people.

The bond of affection between him and his uncle had never been overly warm. But it was a bond, all the same. And now it was irrevocably damaged.

Daniel tried to push these thoughts away. But they returned again and again, like an incoming tide.

Mainwaring sat across from Daniel, dipping his quill pen in a bottle of India ink and scratching away in the ship's log, occupying his mind in his own way. Overhead a yellow lantern light cast an eerie glow on everything. A warm tropical breeze rifted through an open porthole, carrying the fetid smell of the docks and the town. Outside a full moon rose over the harbor, casting a silvery light on the water and land.

Just then, there was a knock on the door.

"Sir?"

It was Mr. Hibbington's voice.

Mainwaring set aside his quill. "Come in," he commanded.

"It's Captain Collins, sir. He's come alongside in a longboat. Says he has an important message for you. Shall I bring him aboard?"

"Of course!" Mainwaring said.

Then Hibbington was gone.

Mainwaring glanced across the table at Daniel.

"Why is he coming here?" Daniel asked. "I thought the

plan was for him and his crew—"

"Never mind all that," Mainwaring said. "Hide yourself, quickly!"

Daniel darted to the closet and settled back into the darkness. He pulled the door closed behind him, crouching down so he could see through the slats.

A moment later, Captain Collins was at the cabin door, yellow in the lantern light. Despite the heat of the evening, he was wearing his woolen Quaker coat, buttoned up to the neck.

Behind Collins, Daniel could see Mr. Hibbington standing on the stairway. He looked as if he wanted to enter the room. But Captain Collins was blocking his way.

"I have a private matter to discuss with thee, Captain," Collins said.

"By all means," Mainwaring said. "You may go now, Hibbington."

The first mate nodded and turned away.

"Shut the door, will you?" Mainwaring asked.

Collins closed the door and stood, towering over Mainwaring.

"Have you brought me news of the pirate?" the officer said urgently.

"Yes," Collins said. "I surely have. I have been with Captain Scarfield. And he asked me to bring thee something."

Collins reached into his coat.

A moment later, Daniel saw Mainwaring staring into the rounded, hollow barrel of a pistol.

CHAPTER ELEVEN

⟨⟨⟨⟨ ⟩⟩⟩⟩

*A*LL DANIEL COULD hear was the creaking of the ship's timbers and the heavy breathing of the two men.

"What is the meaning of this?" Mainwaring said at last.

"I promised I would bring you face to face with Scarfield, didn't I?"

"Yes," Mainwaring said warily. "Where is he?"

Collins leaned forward, his eyes cold and hard in the lantern light. With his free hand, he slowly unfastened the buttons down the front of his Quaker coat. When the flaps fell aside, Daniel could see that his uncle was wearing a broad bandolier across his chest. In the leather loops were six deadly-looking pistols.

"No," Mainwaring said shakily. "It can't be—"

Collins gave a low, murderous laugh. "Yes," he declared. "I am Captain Jack Scarfield, sure enough. Look at me, James Mainwaring, if you want to see a pirate!"

He drew a second pistol and leveled both at Mainwaring's face.

Daniel felt a shock race down his spine. He was too stunned to breathe. He crouched, still as a statue, straining to hear every word.

Daniel saw the blood drain from Mainwaring's face. He already looked like a dead man.

"Many people trusted you," Mainwaring said through clenched teeth. "And you have betrayed them all. It was hard enough to picture you trading with the pirates. But I never imagined you would sink to their level. And to think you once preached to me about the purity of the soul—"

The pirate laughed.

"Purity has its rewards, James Mainwaring. And so does boldness. There is a time for each. There is a time to be Collins and a time to be Scarfield. But I would not expect you to understand that. For you, it is all so simple: right and wrong, black and white, rich and poor.

"That is because you have not seen what I have seen: You have not witnessed men being chained and whipped in the fields or children torn from the arms of their mothers on the auction block! You have not heard goat-bearded elders filling the Meeting House with their pious words about the scourge of slavery, even as they grow the grain that feeds these slave-infested islands! Even as they invest in the sugar fields that require the labor of kidnapped children! Even as they enjoy the goods of these Godforsaken isles!

"The rum bottle that sits on the table beside you is a product of someone's suffering in the cane fields. Its pleasant taste is flavored with their sweat and blood. Do you know that? Do you think about that? No, I am sure you do not.

"It may surprise you, James Mainwaring, to know that many of the men aboard my ship were once bound men in the cane thickets. They are now free, free to chart their own courses and make their own fortunes!"

"Free to maim and murder," Mainwaring corrected.

The pirate raised his pistols until they were just inches from Mainwaring's head. The oiled barrels gleamed in the lantern light.

"I have had enough of your sanctimonious chatter. One way or the other," the pirate declared, "I will take this ship. But I would prefer to take her in a peaceable manner, just as your old friend, Captain Collins, would have wanted, without a shot fired or a drop of blood spilled.

"This is the plan: You will call your first mate and order him to throw down the rope ladders and prepare to receive our boarding party. Tell him we are laying an ambush for Scarfield, if you like. Then, when my men are on your deck, we will outnumber you two to one. One signal from me, and in the blink of an eye, this ship will be ours."

"And if I refuse?" Mainwaring said.

"Then I will fire one of these pistols and my men will swarm aboard, hacking your crew to pieces. Believe me, they would much prefer this approach. Once they have their blood worked up, they are very hard to restrain. The choice is yours: life or death. What say you?"

Mainwaring straightened his back. "As long as there is blood running in my veins, you will not have this ship."

Scarfield shook his head. "Very well, James Mainwaring," the pirate spat out. "You have just signed your own death warrant—"

Daniel heard Scarfield thumb back the hammers on both pistols.

Before he knew what he was doing, Daniel was on his feet, pulling his pistol from his belt and shouldering his way into the room.

As soon as the closet door creaked open, Scarfield gave a savage cry and whirled in Daniel's direction. For one terrible moment, their eyes met. The boy saw a flicker of recognition and then a wave of astonishment cross his uncle's face.

Daniel raised his gun. He willed his finger to tighten on the trigger. But his hand would not obey him. It was as if someone had snipped the lines between his brain and his body.

Daniel heard Scarfield bellow in rage. He saw the ugly snout of the buccaneer's pistol coming up, thrusting in his direction like the head of a deadly viper. His body felt numb, as if it belonged to someone else. His gun was as useless as a piece of wood.

He closed his eyes and waited for the blast to tear him apart.

But it did not come. Instead he heard the sound of shattering glass, then an astonished groan. When he opened his eyes, he saw Scarfield sinking heavily to his knees. As the big man fell, both his pistols went off, blowing a hole in the ceiling above Daniel's head.

The tiny cabin was suddenly filled with showering splinters and blue smoke.

Daniel lost his balance and fell backward against the cabin wall.

He squinted through the haze, and there, standing over the body of the twitching pirate, was James Mainwaring. In his hand was the neck of the shattered rum bottle. And at his feet, blood was pumping fast from a hole in the back of the pirate's head.

For an instant, Daniel and the officer simply stared at each other, wild-eyed, their ears ringing, their breath coming fast and shallow in the smoky room.

Then, from overhead, they heard the crack of musket fire and the pounding of running feet.

"We're being boarded!" Mainwaring said hoarsely. He snatched up his cutlass and a freshly primed pistol from the rack over the table. In a moment, he was gone.

Daniel knew what he must do. He must follow Mainwaring to the deck. With shaking hands, he turned to the closet to find his sword. It was then he noticed that he was standing in a pool of shimmering blood—his family's blood. Daniel knelt and touched his fingers to the glistening hole in his uncle's scalp. He knew he should be on deck, with the others. But he could not bring himself to leave his uncle to bleed to death on the floor.

Daniel pulled his shirt over his head and tore it into three pieces. Then he fell on his knees, pressing the wadded cloth to the wound.

While the sounds of battle thundered above him, Daniel knelt on the splintered floor, cradling his uncle's head in his lap. The yellow lantern swayed wildly above them, casting weird shadows. Captain Collins' eyes were half-open, but were dull as balls of glass, staring at nothing. Daniel bent and held his ear close to the man's mouth. He detected a feeble tremor of breath.

At last, when he was satisfied that he had stopped the worst of the bleeding, Daniel wrapped the bandage tightly, fashioning the cloth into a turban.

Just then, he heard a terrible scream. Daniel looked up in time to see a half-naked body fall headlong down the gang-way and sprawl, open-mouthed, in the swaying light. He was young and slim, not much older than Daniel himself.

Daniel stared at the intruder. But the pirate did not move. He was dead as yesterday's supper. When he looked more closely, he saw that the back of the boy's head was missing.

Seeing a boy his own age die so suddenly shook him to the core.

Daniel knew if he did not make his way up onto the deck, the attackers would eventually find him and he would die here in this small room, beside his uncle's body. At least on the deck, in the open air, he would have a fighting chance.

Taking a deep breath, he drew his weapons and crept up the rough wooden stairs, toward the battle.

Nothing could have prepared him for the sight that greeted him on deck. The ship was solid with men, swing-ing their weapons and firing their pistols. There were pirates everywhere, leaping into the gun pits, hacking with their swords, and firing into the faces of Mainwaring's men.

Overhead they were in the rigging, setting fire to the sails. The canvas burned with a ferocious roaring sound, like an approaching hurricane. Great chunks of sailcloth ripped loose and fell, dropping on the fighting men below.

In the bloody tangle of the main deck, a forest of waving swords and axes clanged against one another in the blue smoke. Everyone was shouting; some men were crying out like wild animals. In the shimmering moonlight, the deck was black with blood.

Sweeping his eyes over the melee, Daniel suddenly caught sight of Killy. He was on the gun deck just below, over by the number-five cannon, armed with a wet blanket, thrashing away at a powder keg that had burst into flames.

Daniel took one step in that direction, just as the cask exploded. The force of the blast knocked Daniel off his feet and sent him hurtling through the air. There was no pain, no time to be afraid, only a great thunderclap and a metallic ringing in his ears.

Suddenly he was lying flat on his back on the rough boards of the deck, staring up at the burning sails. He lifted his hands and saw that, miraculously, they were still attached to his arms. Even more surprising, he had managed to hold on to his weapons.

Daniel rolled to his feet, his nostrils stinging. All was muffled silence. The crack of the gunfire and the thump of the explosions sounded very far away. The beating of his heart and laboring of his own lungs were all he heard.

Then he saw Killy, lying on his side by the cannon, his body splotched with powder burns. Daniel set his weapons down and crawled on all fours to the carpenter. He grabbed him by the ankles and dragged him into the shelter of an overturned lifeboat.

Moving in this silent world, he went down on hands and knees and crawled back through the smoke to retrieve his weapons. But as he reached out for his sword, he felt something crush down on his hand, pinning it to the deck.

At first, all he saw was a heavy boot. But when he raised his eyes, he found himself looking up into the face of the Man with the Silver Oar.

Daniel blinked to make sure that he wasn't imagining things. But, no, it was the man all right. The death-bringer peered down through the sulphurous blue smoke, grim and remote.

He was dressed in the same crimson coat and wore the same white powdered wig under a tricornered hat. Balanced on his shoulder was the long oar, slanting up into the moonlight. He was moving his lips, but Daniel could not make out what he was saying.

Just then, there was another explosion by the number-seven gun. Daniel felt the thump off to his right. He ducked as a shower of splintered wood rained down all around him. The boot lifted from his hand. When he looked up, the Man with the Silver Oar was gone.

Daniel rose to his feet. Then he saw him moving like a silken apparition among the dead and dying: a hand, an arm, that pale death-skull of a face appearing now and again through the blue smoke. Soon he had disappeared entirely.

Fires were burning everywhere now. Daniel sheathed his sword and stuck his pistol in his belt. The only fighting he would do now would be with the blanket and the bucket, which were laid ready by the gun pits. With Killy lying like a dead man, he knew the firefighting was left to him. He dipped his blanket in a bucket of water and ducked into the billowing smoke toward the number-seven gun.

This was dangerous work. Many of the gun crews had been driven back from their positions, leaving their sacks of gunpowder lying on the deck. Daniel crawled through the wreckage, dragging the explosives back from the edge of the flames.

The fighting was thick around him. The exhausted men on the main deck, grappling in the smoke and the clashing steel, struggled to stay alive for one moment longer. Burning sackcloth rained from above, scorching everything it touched.

Many times, Daniel came within a hairbreadth of being struck by a sword blade or gutted by a flying musket ball. But each time, instinct made him crouch or duck and whirl just in time to miss the deathblow.

It seemed that hours passed this way, in the smoke and noise. Wave after wave of pirates came over the gunwales until Mainwaring's men were greatly outnumbered.

Once, while crouched on the quarterdeck, Daniel saw a powerful, dark-haired man climbing hand-over-hand up a rope thirty feet above him. He flashed back to the day of the hanging. He wondered: Was it possible that Moses Skellington was here, in the midst of the fight? But before he could get a better look at him, the climber was lost in the smoke of the battle.

Daniel shook his head. He was seeing things, he told himself. If he were going to survive the night, he would have to keep his wits about him.

Daniel was overwhelmed by the number of men crowded onto the deck. How had they all fit on Scarfield's ship?

Then, with a terrible certainty, he understood: This was not just Scarfield's crew. The sounds of the battle had attracted other pirates. Like sharks drawn to the scent of blood, they too had come for the kill, some climbing aboard to join the fight, some waiting in the shadows to ravage the vessel when the smoke cleared.

But, as bad as the pirates were, the fire was just as deadly an enemy. The roaring flames were spreading rapidly, consuming everything that would burn. Daniel was fighting the blaze alone. He would have given anything to have his companion by his side at this moment. When the munitions stacked around the cannons began to detonate, the ship became a floating bomb. The reverberations could be heard from one end of the harbor to the other.

The explosives were going off in rapid succession, blowing men and debris high into the air. The water around the ship became a floating junkyard of charred bodies and shattered wreckage.

On the starboard rail, Daniel saw a handful of pirates retreating, leaping overboard to escape the deadly explosions. At amidships, more of the marauders followed, in ragged clusters of three and four. Within moments, Daniel saw the tide of the battle turn. Afraid the ship would sink, the pirates dropped their weapons and the rails were filled with frightened men, vaulting overboard and plunging into the choppy ocean.

Daniel considered following them, thinking he might be safer in the water. But he could not bring himself to abandon ship as long as his comrades were still aboard.

Just when it seemed that flames would consume the *Sea Turtle*, a knot of marines appeared through the smoke on the main deck, armed with buckets dipped from the sea. They doused the crackling deck boards, beating the fire back into the shadows. Daniel pushed ahead and joined them, helping them smother the scorching blaze.

A dozen of the *Sea Turtle*'s most nimble sailors clenched knives in their teeth and climbed into the rigging, hacking away at the lines that held the burning sails in place. When the great canvas sheets came tumbling down, they kicked them into the sea, where they hissed and belched smoke, rolling in the black water like sea serpents.

Daniel rose, blanket in hand, and squinted through the blue haze. His hearing was coming back now. For the first time, he allowed himself to think he might live through this battle.

Lanterns were glowing on every ship in the harbor. The other buccaneers were awake, sure enough. Daniel knew they were watching, watching and waiting, to see who would win this deadly contest, waiting like carrion crows to come and pick over the spoils.

But they would not come now, he was sure of that. The explosions had made the *Sea Turtle* the deadliest spot on the harbor, and even the most foolish pirate would not risk venturing near until the fires were snuffed out.

A swath of purple clouds closed around the moon, smothering it until it was just a pale puff of light in the night sky.

Aboard the *Sea Turtle*, all was quiet and creaking. The

dead were still. The living were moving slowly, as if in a dream.

Daniel slumped against the mast. Suddenly he felt very tired. Carefully he laid his sodden, charred blanket on the deck. He closed his eyes. He would rest, he told himself, for just a moment, and then he would rise and find Captain Mainwaring and Killy. He would do his duty. But for now, he simply wanted to rest. He shut his stinging eyes and plunged into a dense, dense fog of sleep.

When the tropical sun burned up over the horizon, Daniel opened his eyes. He did not know where he was. He was immediately aware of the caked blood blocking his ears and nostrils and the stench of smoke that clung to everything. All around him, the deck was abuzz with bluebottle flies, crawling on openmouthed corpses and cavorting in the glistening pools of blood.

Overhead the vultures circled low. They swooped down, folding their dark wings before perching on the lifeless bodies and setting to work with their sharp beaks and claws. One bold scavenger touched down at Daniel's side and pecked at the cloth of his bloody sleeve. Daniel gave a cry of indignation and shoved the bird away.

"I'm not yours yet," he said fiercely.

Daniel sat up. He was relieved to see that he was not the only survivor. He could see that while he lay sprawled on the deck like a dead man, the able-bodied seamen had been up and at work. Sailors were up in the shrouds, replacing the sails and repairing the severed rigging. Others were hauling away the ruined spars and tossing the splintered deck boards over the rail.

The tangled heaps of corpses had already begun to putrefy in the warm tropical air. The marines went from man to man, looking for signs of life. When they found a fallen comrade, they laid him on his back, with a handkerchief covering his face. They carried the wounded onto the upper deck where Doctor Esquemeling had set up a field hospital. The good doctor worked with grim determination, his surgeon's apron spattered with gore, his shirtsleeves bloody to the elbows.

As for the pirates, the marines slit the throats of the wounded and tossed both the dead and dying overboard. The deckhands were hauling up buckets of seawater and sloshing the deck clean. The bloodied water ran so thickly down the sides of the *Sea Turtle* that the ocean around the ship turned the color of rose wine. The sand sharks began to arrive, darting about the wreckage in a feeding frenzy.

Mainwaring had survived the fight. Daniel could see him on the upper deck, along with his officers, directing the repairs. But he could not see any sign of Killy. Daniel's eyes rested on the rows of dead, laid out neatly on the deck. He prayed that the carpenter was not among them.

Daniel forced himself to stand and make his way across the length of the ship, stepping over the rubble. No one said a word to him. It was as if he were a ghost. He knelt by the dead, lifting the stained kerchiefs and peering into the faces of his crewmates. Their skin was waxen and cold to the touch. Their hair, still wet with salt spray and blood, was plastered to their faces. But it was their eyes that haunted him the most. They were flattened and dull, like coins that had passed through too many hands and had been taken out of circulation by some divine bookkeeper.

Then Daniel heard a familiar voice behind him say, "Come away from there, lad." He turned and there, standing in the morning light, was Killy, his skin splotched with powder burns.

"You're alive," Daniel managed.

"Aye," Killy said, placing a hand on his shoulder. "We're alive, lad, to fight another day."

Overhead the vultures were circling closer. On the upper deck, Mr. Buckthorn was piping the men to work. Daniel and Killy went to find their tools. They had to get the *Sea Turtle* shipshape. Daniel knew they must leave the Devil's island, and quickly, before the circling wolves in the harbor gathered the courage to come for their share.

CHAPTER TWELVE

⁓ ᦚ ⁓

MANY PIRATES DIED on the decks of the *Sea Turtle* that night. But Jack Scarfield was not among them. He still clung to life, by a slender thread.

When Daniel finally returned to Mainwaring's cabin, he saw that his uncle had been moved to Mainwaring's bunk. Dr. Esquemeling was at his side, winding a fresh bandage around his head. His chest was lifting, his breathing fast and shallow. His eyes were sunken in the familiar face that Daniel had known for so long, the face of a man who had led an astonishing double life.

Mainwaring was bent over his table, studying a nautical chart, when Daniel appeared in the doorway.

Mainwaring stood and extended his hand, gravely. "I want to thank you," the officer said, "for saving my life and the lives of every man jack on this ship. I will see that you are richly rewarded. If you want a career in the navy, it's yours."

"Thank you, sir," Daniel managed. "But I can't think about any of that now."

Daniel could see that Mainwaring's face was pale and

drawn. The jaunty smile was gone. The long night and the prospect of an even longer day had taken a toll.

Daniel wanted to thank the officer for saving his life as well. But he could not put the words together. Instead he cast a sidelong glance at the wounded man.

"How is Uncle—I mean—what shall I call him?"

Mainwaring sighed. "I suppose he will always be your uncle. But he is also an enemy of the Crown. And as much as I can appreciate your confusion, it is my duty to bring him in. I will bring him back alive, if I can. He may never recover fully. But they can hang him tied to a chair, if necessary."

"He's a tough old bird," Dr. Esquemeling said. "Any ordinary man would have been killed by the blow you gave this fellow. He's got a hole in his skull the size of a walnut."

"Let's not dwell on the past," Mainwaring said abruptly. "We must set sail as soon as we are able. We are in an extremely exposed position. Every hour we remain here places us in even greater danger. And I do not know that we could survive another battle.

"Mister Buckthorn assures me that he can have our ship ready to sail in a matter of hours. But before we can slip away, we must deal with the pirate ship. If my suspicions are correct, your uncle's vessel contains a fortune in stolen goods. The investors are counting on us to bring back whatever we can.

"I am setting up a party to board the ship. I need you to go along. Anything you can tell us about your uncle's habits might be helpful. There might even be documents leading us to buried treasure somewhere ashore. We will not leave until we have searched the cabin completely. Then, when we have stripped her of everything we can use, we will burn her and slip away from this wretched place."

Daniel swallowed. "Burn her?" he gasped.

"Well, of course, just as I have many others. Otherwise she will just end up in the hands of another pirate. What's wrong?"

"You can't burn her," Daniel said.

"Excuse me?"

"The ship is mine," Daniel said. "It was my grandfather's ship, and my father's as well."

Mainwaring smiled impatiently. "I am afraid that no longer matters, Daniel. That ship is a pirate vessel—"

"I cannot allow you to burn her," Daniel repeated, surprised at how strong his voice sounded. Then, before Mainwaring could overcome his astonishment, a thought flitted through Daniel's brain, like a colorful island bird.

"Wait a moment," the boy said. "Captain, it just occurred to me: How will we prove that we have actually completed our mission?"

"We have the pirate," Mainwaring said, nodding in the direction of the dying man.

"No, we do not," Daniel countered. "What we have is the body of Elias Collins, one of Philadelphia's most respected business leaders. No investor will want my uncle's blood on his hands. Unless this is handled properly, you could find yourself in the midst of a terrible scandal."

"I have the testimony of Doctor Esquemeling and my officers," Mainwaring said confidently. "That will be sufficient to clear up any confusion. It is a bizarre story, I will admit, but once the facts are out in the open—"

Daniel nodded. "That may be," he said. "But let's come back to the issue that launched this expedition in the first place."

"And what might that be?"

"Captain Mainwaring," Daniel said, "surely you haven't forgotten about Scarfield's treasure?"

Mainwaring narrowed his eyes. "What do you know about your uncle's treasure?" he asked.

"I don't know any more than you do," Daniel admitted. "But I do know this: Somewhere aboard that ship is the key to understanding the mystery of my uncle's life. And that knowledge will lead us to the fortune. Are you with me so far?"

"Go on."

"We have every reason to believe Scarfield has amassed tremendous wealth. I don't think you will discover Scarfield's secrets in a hasty search. And if you burn the ship, any chance of recovering the treasure will go up in flames."

Mainwaring was silent for a moment.

"You see that I'm right," Daniel ventured.

"Perhaps," Mainwaring said at last. "A thorough search of the ship might reveal many things: maps to buried treasure or an island hideout, possibly an indigo plantation tucked away deep in the interior. The investors might see the burning as a rash move."

"I believe it would be very rash, Captain," Daniel said. "I

know that you and your backers will want to profit from this venture. And you have every right to be rewarded for your efforts.

"I, on the other hand, do not want to watch my family's ship go up in flames. This is what I propose: I will give you and your crew legal right to any treasure or maps you can find aboard the *Good Samaritan*—provided you will escort me and my craft safely back to Philadelphia."

Mainwaring stared at his boots for a moment. Then he nodded. "You have a deal, my young hero. I will send that party over immediately. Once we are assured that there are no pirates aboard, we will tow the ship out of the harbor.

"When we are clear of these islands, we shall drop anchor and conduct a preliminary search. Then we will make the *Good Samaritan* shipshape and sail her back to Philadelphia as you have directed. We certainly have enough men to pilot the craft.

"You are correct. There is no real advantage in destroying her. It might even be safer making the return trip with two ships rather than one. When we arrive at Penns Landing, I will expect your complete cooperation. Is this agreeable?"

Daniel nodded. "Yes, Captain," he said.

Mainwaring reached out and shook his hand. "You have a good head on your shoulders, Daniel," he said. "I am glad you did not lose it to a cannonball."

"Thank you, sir. May I go now?"

Mainwaring laughed. "Yes, of course. There is much to do!"

Daniel left the cabin, shaken by the thought that he had

come so close to losing the ship. He had used his head, sure enough, and his uncle's ship would soon be his!

As busy as he and Killy were, putting the ship back in shape, Daniel did take notice when the marines rowed over to the *Good Samaritan* and scrambled aboard. There were several pistol shots as they finished off the wounded pirates who still lurked on deck. Then all was still and quiet aboard the bloodstained ship. In the morning light, Daniel could see that the pirate ship truly did have red sails, which had been raised during the night. The Jolly Roger lifted in the wind at the topmast.

The *Sea Turtle* and the *Good Samaritan* were on the open sea within an hour, leaving the treacherous harbor behind them, floating with wreckage. With the pirate ship hauled behind her, the *Sea Turtle* sailed north for several hours, until Mainwaring gave orders to drop anchor well off the coast.

Then Daniel and Mainwaring climbed into a longboat and were rowed across to the ship.

"Tell me this," Mainwaring asked, as the oarsmen pulled hard through the ocean swells, "have you ever been aboard your uncle's ship?"

Daniel shook his head. "No. For reasons I understand now, I was forbidden to set foot on the *Good Samaritan*. In fact, Uncle was always very particular on that point. No one other than his crew could come aboard her. Even his most trusted associates were not permitted on her deck. He said he considered it his sanctuary and would not have it invaded by idle curiosity seekers."

"Well," Mainwaring said, "You can board her now."

They came alongside. The ship looked smaller, close up. Daniel guessed she was maybe fifty feet from bow to stern. He estimated that her deck was a mere twenty-feet wide and her hold less than ten-feet deep. She sat low in the water and carried her sails on two graceful masts.

The party went up the rope ladder. Once on deck, Daniel immediately noticed the cannons—there were six of them, hidden behind the gun ports, where no outside observer would ever detect them.

The tools of war were everywhere: The deck was strewn with sabers and pistols and battle axes, boxes of grenades and bundles of torches, drums and trumpets, rolls of bandages, and glass bottles of rum and medicine. Beneath her peaceful-looking façade, the *Good Samaritan* was a floating fortress.

Daniel went along with Mainwaring's men as they began a complete search of the ship, bow to stern, top to bottom. Furled and heaped on the deck, they found the white sails Collins had used during his more peaceful interludes.

Down in the hold, they found a wooden box of flags of many nationalities. They also discovered a wide strip of canvas, which was designed to be hung over the bow of the ship, to cover the name of the *Good Samaritan*. The large black letters on the banner formed the grisly name, the *Revenge*. In their haste, Scarfield's men had forgotten to hang it.

The decks below were in even greater disarray. Daniel was

amazed at the accumulation of gaudy trash that was piled high: colorful clothing and crockery and basketry, overflowing with baubles and cheap jewelry.

The crew's quarters were especially offensive. The low-ceilinged room looked as if it had been hit by a hurricane. The floor was ankle deep in putrid garbage and empty rum bottles. Discarded pieces of clothing were lying everywhere.

The carcass of a fish, half-eaten and buzzing with flies, lay on a copper plate on the main table. An antler-handled knife was thrust savagely into the arm of one of the chairs, and weapons lay casually on every surface, ready to be clutched at a moment's notice.

Daniel was grateful when they made their way up into the open air toward the captain's cabin, which dominated the upper deck of the ship, well to the rear.

The wooden door creaked as Daniel pushed it open. A shaft of tropical light streamed through the doorway, where dust danced in the air.

It was strange, after all these years, to step into the heart of his uncle's secret world.

The cabin was immaculate. The floor was clean, the brass was polished, and everything was in its place. An entire wall of the cabin was solid with ledger books, neatly arranged on the sea-sturdy shelves. It was a sanctuary of sanity in the midst of so much filth and bloodshed.

Daniel took down one of the black ledgers and sat in his uncle's chair. He scanned the precise columns, which carried an inventory list of flour and cornmeal. He recognized his uncle's steady, sober handwriting.

At once he thought of Terra and Hettie and the well-ordered life back on Spruce Street. It was difficult to believe the same man who made these careful entries could have written the cruel, taunting note that Mainwaring discovered at the first shipwreck, weeks ago.

Then a shadow fell through the doorway, blocking the sunlight.

"Have you found anything of interest?" Mainwaring asked.

Daniel closed the book.

"Yes, sir," he said quietly.

"Any clues to the location of the treasure?"

"Not yet, sir."

"Well, keep looking—it's critical."

Then he looked around.

"Had a penchant for neatness, didn't he?" the officer said.

"Yes, sir."

"Oh, by the way, we have a prisoner. A black man they cornered and captured down in the hold. He's talking a blue streak, but no one can understand him. Charley Boatknife is being brought over. He can speak a bit of the Spanish. Maybe that will work."

Before Daniel could say anything more, two marines dragged the black man into the room and pushed him roughly onto the floor. He lay there trembling, tears in his eyes, mumbling incomprehensible words.

Daniel looked away. He took down another ledger, one with a red leather cover, and began to page through it. This one was different. This was not an inventory of goods, but of men, hundreds of men. The columns were filled with unpronounceable names. The notations were in his uncle's hand. But Daniel could not make any sense of it.

Before long, Boatknife appeared in the doorway. Daniel could see he had a nasty cut over his left eye and a bruise along the jawline, but he seemed to be moving nimbly enough. He sat down on the floor by the captive and began talking slowly, soothingly.

The black man sat up and stared into the faces of his captors. He gestured to the ledgers and talked loudly, becoming more and more agitated.

Charley just nodded occasionally, his eyes wide with wonder.

At last, the man stopped speaking. It was as if he had exhausted himself. He stared at the floor beneath him.

"Well, sir," Charley said, "seems that there's more to this Captain Scarfield than meets the eye. He was able to switch back and forth, either disguisin' himself as a merchant or takin' to the red sails and becomin' a pirate. He'd cruise the coastline, waylayin' ships, murderin' and robbin' as he went. But all the while, he carried a reg'lar cargo. He played both ends against the middle, ya see. When he arrived here in the islands, he would sell off his flour and cornmeal to the highest bidder, jest like a reg'lar trader."

Mainwaring shifted impatiently.

"What's so unusual about that?" he demanded.

"Well, sir, he had a curious habit of meetin' the slave ships when they brought a load of poor prisoners over from Africa. He'd be all pious and Quakerlike, with his ship and crew lookin' scrubbed up like a buncha angels. And darned if he wouldn't use the money from his plunderin' to buy the slaves' freedom."

Mainwaring looked at Daniel in amazement. But Charley went on. "But, sir, here's the kicker: He'd switch back into his piratin' garb, hoist the red sails and run down the slavers as they left the harbor. He'd take 'em by storm and steal the money right back from 'em! So it seems like he used his piracy to liberate these men and set 'em free to farm or wander or become pirates themselves if they chose to be!

"This fella says he's been with Scarfield for three years. Came over on a slaver from the west coast of Africa, got set free at the docks of Santo Domingo and has stuck to the captain like glue ever since. I didn't have the heart to tell him the old bird'll prob'ly be dead by nightfall."

Mainwaring peered into the black man's face. "Thank you, Boatknife. You may return to your duty station. Oh, and before you do, be sure to tell this man that he is my prisoner. He may have information that will prove very helpful in the future."

Charley cast his eyes down and made a swift translation.

The man's face fell. Then he rose up to his full height, pushing past the marines and sprinting for the rail. In seconds, he was over the side, diving headfirst into the water and swimming for the distant islands as if his life depended upon it.

"Stop him!" Mainwaring shouted.

One of the marines unslung his musket and leaned down to shoot the man in the back. But Daniel rushed up beside him and knocked the barrel aside just as the marine pulled the trigger. The ball hit the water a dozen feet from where the man had entered.

"Let him go!" Daniel urged. "My uncle set him free. We've got no call to change that."

The marine looked back at Mainwaring with slitted eyes.

"I want that man," the captain said. "Go after him!"

The marines dropped into a boat. But before they could even set the oars to the locks, he was gone, vanished like a fish in the choppy ocean.

They circled the boat twice but found nothing.

Mainwaring watched it all with a grim face.

He turned to Daniel.

"I could put you in chains for what you just did," he declared. "That was insubordination and interference in the most outrageous manner."

Daniel straightened his back, bracing himself.

The marines stepped closer.

Then, to the boy's surprise, Mainwaring laughed and clapped him on the back.

"I admire your convictions, Daniel. Despite everything, you're still a Quaker, aren't you?"

"Yes," Daniel said quietly. "I suppose I am."

Mainwaring turned to the men clustered around them.

"All right," he said. "The excitement is over. Let's continue searching. I want the ship turned inside out!"

The marines turned slowly and went about their work, casting dark looks in the boy's direction.

Mainwaring glanced sideways at Daniel.

"Don't look so scared," he said. "I don't think that man would have told us much anyway. He was loyal to your uncle, any fool could see that."

"Captain," Daniel said, "may I speak freely?"

"You may."

"I still can't get over the idea that Uncle Elias had everyone so completely fooled. I admit, he was not an easy person to know. But I thought I knew—"

"You only knew a part of him," Mainwaring said. "Many maritime men lead double lives, being one person while in port and another at sea. It is more common than you might think. I am not suggesting that he was always a criminal. I am sure he started out as honest as the next man.

"It may have begun very gradually: Once he became master of his own ship, after your father was gone, perhaps he yielded to the temptation to smuggle or run contraband. Many men do. He may have drifted in and out of the criminal world, changing identities when it suited his purpose. With the aid of a loyal crew, it was possible for the pirate and the merchant to exist, side by side."

Daniel recalled the strange transformation he had seen his uncle undergo when he spoke at Quaker meeting. If a man was so open to the voices of the angels, could he also fall prey to the voices of demons?

Daniel sighed. Perhaps this was as close as he would ever come to an explanation. Daniel did not share these thoughts with Mainwaring. Daniel knew that Mainwaring, for all of his quick-wittedness, was not a man inclined to self-examination. He was not a spiritual pilgrim or a seeker of mystical realms. He did not ponder anything beyond the next reward, the next mission, the next new horizon.

Mainwaring and his men spent the entire day searching the ship. But for all their effort, they did not find any maps or treasure. The decks were a cluttered wasteland of broken and useless things. The hold contained nothing more exciting than barrels of flour and heaps of colorful refuse.

By sundown, the deckhands had tossed the trash overboard and completed all the essential repairs to the ship's sails and rigging. Mainwaring ordered Mr. Hibbington to select a crew of a dozen sailors to sail the *Good Samaritan* back to Philadelphia. They would chart a course for Florida in the morning.

When the seamen arrived, their first act was to cut down the bloodred sails and toss them into the ocean. Then they hoisted the white sheets and spread them before the wind.

Before he headed back to the *Sea Turtle* for his things, Daniel sprang into the rigging and climbed to the highest mast. He unsheathed his sword and cut the rope holding the Black Flag in place. He meant to take the flag back as evidence of their strange capture. But as he climbed down, the wind caught the banner and tore it free. He watched as it tumbled away on the trade winds, dipping low over the ocean, where it was swallowed by a wave and sank without a trace.

That evening, when he returned to the *Sea Turtle*, Daniel went straight to Mainwaring's cabin. He wanted to look into his uncle's eyes once again.

He half expected to find a corpse. But he did not. His uncle lingered on, in a feverish delirium. Daniel sat up by his bedside, keeping a curious vigil.

The evening meal came and went. But Daniel had no appetite for food. Exhaustion overtook him. While his uncle was resting peacefully, he made his way to his own hammock, telling himself that he would lie down for just a few minutes. But as soon as he slumped into the canvas sling, he fell into a deep sleep that lasted for hours.

At one point in the night, Daniel found himself again at his uncle's bedside, staring into the calm face of Elias Collins.

"I would like to die now," Captain Collins said, looking blankly at the ceiling. "But I would prefer to do it out under the open sky."

Whether it was a prayer or a request, Daniel could not tell, but it was uttered in such a moderate, well-measured way that Daniel felt compelled to comply. He called Dr. Esquemeling and, with help from a few of the marines, they lifted the dying man and carried him onto the upper deck, where he would have a clear view of the watery world he had once commanded.

Daniel watched Collins sit up and run a trembling hand over the bandage that covered his head.

"He'll come for me now," Collins said. "By God, he'll come for me, and there is not a thing I can do about it."

"Who will come for you?" Daniel asked.

But his uncle did not answer.

Then, moving with painful slowness, he knelt there on the deck and prayed, moving his lips in a conversation not meant for human ears. The marines crouched nearby, watching everything with curious eyes. But the doctor chased them off a good distance, saying something about letting the Quaker captain "die in peace."

Daniel turned to Dr. Esquemeling and saw that the surgeon's eyes were wide with amazement. Dr. Esquemeling pointed toward the west.

"Look there," he said.

Daniel could clearly see the flash of oars on the water: a single oarsman in an open boat on the tossing waves. And as he came closer, Daniel took in a sharp breath. It was the messenger of death, coming straight for the *Sea Turtle*. With each dip of the silver oars, the boat surged closer.

The Man with the Silver Oar brought his boat to within a few yards of the *Sea Turtle* then stowed his oars and sat, waiting, the boat tossing quietly on the waves.

Daniel noticed that his uncle had gone limp now. His faced seemed almost peaceful, as if he were drifting off into a comfortable sleep. The surgeon nodded to the marines. Without a word, they dropped a rope around the sea captain's shoulders, cinched it tight, and lowered him over the side.

The man sat bolt upright on the seat, his oars at his side, surveying the dangling man from under the brim of his hat. When Collins was settled into the boat, the marines tossed the rope down. It landed in a coil beside the body.

Silently the mysterious man set his oars into the water.

Daniel heard the eerie creak of the oarlocks and saw the flashing of the silver oars against the dark of the ocean. A cold shiver crept up his spine and lifted the hairs at the base of his neck.

For as long as his eyes would let him, Daniel watched the boat disappear into the blackness. Then, at last, there was nothing more to see. What had once been a point of silvery light was swallowed by the heaving dark of the ocean. An unseasonable chill lay across the water.

Suddenly a rough hand was shaking Daniel awake. When he opened his eyes, he was surprised to find himself aboard the *Sea Turtle*, in the darkness of the carpenter's cabin, slumped in his swaying hammock.

"I been lookin' for you high and low," Killy said, close to his ear. "Just so you know, your uncle died an hour ago."

Daniel blinked, scarcely able to believe what he was hearing. "He's dead?"

"Aye, lad. And much the better for it, if you ask me. The doctor said he passed away like a babe in its sleep. I wish you coulda been there."

"I was, Killy." Daniel said. "I was there, sure enough."

The carpenter looked at him quizzically.

But Daniel knew there was no way to explain.

The next morning, Daniel packed his sea bag and left Killy in the carpenter's cabin. For the rest of the voyage, he would stay aboard the *Good Samaritan*.

"Thanks for watching over me," Daniel said to the carpenter.

"Aye, you're a good one, sure enough, Dan. That first day you were up and about, when I saw you make that climb through the riggin', I knew then that you were solid stuff. You've got the sea in your blood, Dan. Don't ever forget that."

"Listen, Killy," Daniel said. "You have given me much advice. But now I would like to return the favor."

"Fair enough. What is it, lad?"

"I think you should get out of this pirate-hunting business," Daniel declared. "It's hot, dirty work and powerfully dangerous. You should find a more dignified position. If I can be so bold, I will ask this: How would you like to serve aboard a merchant trading ship? I know a vessel owner who's going to need a good carpenter."

Killy rubbed a rough hand across the reddish stubble of his chin.

"Maybe so," he said, "but don't forget: We still have fifteen hundred miles of deep water to navigate before we are snug in the wharf at Penn's Landing. When we're safe and sound on Billy Penn's ground, we'll have us a dram and talk about it."

Daniel nodded. "Right enough, Mister Killington. I'll speak with you then."

Before Daniel left to join his new crew, Dr. Esquemeling and Captain Mainwaring stood with him at the rail as the marines lowered his uncle's body over the side and into the heaving ocean. When they released the line, the body spun away and sank quickly.

Daniel thought he should whisper a prayer. But then he decided to let him go in silence, like the solitary Quaker he was, to meet his Maker.

When Daniel took possession of the *Good Samaritan*, he felt as if a part of him that had been missing for a very long time had been restored. He walked up and down the length of the ship, knowing that his father's hand and eye had rested on every inch of the good craft. He felt at home at the wheel and up in the rigging. But he could not bring himself to move into the cabin. Instead he slept under a tarpaulin on the upper deck, marveling at the star-sprinkled nights as they headed north, with the *Sea Turtle* as an escort, toward the coastline of North America, homeward bound.

EPILOGUE

⌐•⌐

$\mathcal{T}$HE RETURN TRIP was accomplished in less than two weeks. The crew scrubbed the ship from top to bottom and threw the pirate rubble into the sea.

During those glorious days, the *Good Samaritan* sailed like a dream, sometimes outrunning the *Sea Turtle*, sometimes tarrying close behind.

Daniel chose to work as a common seaman, taking his turn with the others, at the watch and at the wheel. In this way, he came to understand the ship in her many moods.

Sometimes, late at night, when the ocean was alive with starlight, Daniel thought he felt the ghost of his grandfather and his long-lost father standing beside him on the upper deck, peering over his shoulder with shining, watchful eyes.

Too soon, the journey was over. Daniel knew there was much to attend to on shore. There were practical matters that required his undivided attention.

The *Good Samaritan* and the *Sea Turtle* sailed into the docks at Penn's Landing on the afternoon of August 26, 1718. A crowd gathered to greet them. Word had been passed up the coastline that the mission had been a success and that Mainwaring had defeated the most dangerous pirate of the age.

When Daniel and Mainwaring arrived at the house on Spruce Street, they received a hero's welcome. Hettie shamelessly kissed Mainwaring on the doorstep. Both Hettie and Terra remarked at how changed Daniel looked, as if he had become a proper man over the summer.

Daniel did not have the heart to tell Terra the whole truth about her husband's death. He delivered the sad news as gently as he could, saying only that Elias Collins had died in a fight with a pirate, which was true.

News soon spread about the success of Mainwaring's mission. Mainwaring concocted a story about how Scarfield had taken over Captain Collins' ship, murdered him, and posed as the good captain to lure innocent traders within cannon range. It was such a good tale that it rapidly passed from one mouth to another and soon became common knowledge. The crew of the *Sea Turtle* was sworn to secrecy under threat of losing their reward for the voyage. A few wild rumors crept out, but the truth about Captain Collins' indiscretions was too implausible for even his bitterest opponents to believe.

Once the *Good Samaritan* was firmly anchored in the river channel, Mainwaring searched the craft repeatedly. But he could never find any of the great fortune he had lusted after.

He had no reason to complain. His share of the reward for Scarfield's capture from Greyling and the investors was more than sufficient to allow him to leave the navy and pursue other interests.

He and Hettie married at the end of the summer and moved away to New York, where they entered the shipping business and became favorites in the city's social circles. Terra was happy to sell the old house on Spruce Street and move with them, leaving Daniel alone in the Quaker city.

But Daniel was not truly alone—he was surrounded by companions. He took a small room close to the waterfront where he could gaze out his window and see his ship anchored in the river.

At summer's end, Daniel set about the satisfying work of having the *Good Samaritan* unloaded and refitted for further adventures. Tuck and Killy took a special pleasure in restoring the vessel to its former glory. They got along well from the start, and Daniel could hardly wait to put to sea with his two friends once his obligations were satisfied.

In the meantime, there was a great deal of work to be done.

While they were clearing out the hold, they made a startling discovery. Tuck was making his way down the gangplank, pushing a large barrel of flour. It rolled down the wharf, gathering speed, and he lost control. There was nothing he could do but leap aside and watch it bump down the ramp and crash into a piling, shattering into a dozen pieces. Then Tuck caught sight of something dark and leathery nestled in the flour.

When Daniel was summoned, he discovered the flour concealed a large cowhide sack, held closed with a drawstring. They opened the sack and discovered a large quantity of Spanish coins. One by one, Daniel, Tuck, and Killy broke open the remaining barrels. To their surprise, each cask contained some plundered treasure: silver and gold coins, precious jewels, and exotic gems from all over the world.

Because this fortune had been obtained through piracy, Daniel could not bring himself to keep it all. He donated much of it to worthy local charities. He reserved a sizeable sum for the care and maintenance of the family ship. And he put away enough to assure that, come what may, he would never again have to work as a carpenter's apprentice.

Daniel had come a long way in a few short months. He had traveled a great distance and seen a great number of terrifying and beautiful things.

He had gone for adventure, sure enough, and had found his fortune as well. But most importantly, Daniel Collins had discovered himself, a treasure that many a rich man goes to his grave without ever attaining.

Daniel spent the frigid Philadelphia winter by the hearth fire in his room, poring over maps and nautical charts, dreaming about the places he would sail in the seasons to come. With Tuck and Killy and a trusted, handpicked crew, he did sail to many of them and saw many strange and wonderful sights.

But the tale of those times and those voyages, well, that is another story . . .

AFTERWORD

～～～

 $\mathcal{T}$ HIS STORY TAKES PLACE during the final years of "The Golden Age of Piracy," which lasted from 1700–1720.

It was a restless and terrible time, when thousands of young men from the lower classes took up the pistol and the sword and went a-pirating, in search of wealth and adventure. It was an attractive alternative to life in the slums or on the tenant farms.

For most, life was short and brutal: The average pirate had a career of less than two years. Many of the young adventurers were hacked down by the sword or dismembered by grapeshot and cannon fire. Others ended their lives on the gallows. Still others died of tropical fevers or drowned in ocean storms.

Those who survived often fritted away their doubloons in the grog shops and gaming houses of the harbor towns, forcing them to go to sea again and again, winning and losing their fortunes many times over.

A lucky few escaped these dangers to become wealthy and respected men, the masters of magnificent houses and sprawling plantations in the lush paradise of the Caribbean. In a single voyage, a young buccaneer could earn more than he could in a lifetime as a common seaman.

The reign of the buccaneers reached its height in 1720, when more than twenty-five hundred pirates ravaged the eastern coast of North America and the treasure-laden ports of the Caribbean Islands.

How could they be so bold and barbarous?

The answer is simple: There was no one to stop them.

In those days, there was no law on the high seas. Once a ship was out of sight of land, she was easy prey.

Consider this urgent plea from the Commander in Chief of Jamaica, who wrote to England's King George in December of 1718:

"I think the pirates daily increase, taking and plundering most ships that are bound to this island. If a sufficient force is not sent to drive them off, our trade must stop."

At last, powerful leaders in Europe and the Americas reached the limit of their patience. In 1718, the British Lord Admiral made the first move by granting American colonies the right to try and hang pirates on their own soil. Until this time, pirates had to be captured and transported to England for trial and execution.

The Lord Admiral also placed heavy prices on the pirates' heads, attracting a cadre of ambitious bounty hunters. Many prominent buccaneers were hunted down and beheaded.

The King issued pardons to any pirate who swore to lay down his arms and surrender his ship. For some, it was an offer too good to refuse.

Strand by strand, the fabric of the Black Flag began to unravel.

By 1723, the war on piracy had produced dramatic results: The number of active pirates was reduced from twenty-five hundred to less than one thousand. By 1726, only two hundred individual pirates remained in operation. Within a few short years, the buccaneers were hunted into extinction.

But before the pirates faded away, they taught the world a lesson.

For a brief time, they established a floating democracy where leaders were elected by common vote and wealth was shared equally. Compensation was paid for injuries sustained in the line of duty, and no man was permitted to cheat the others of their rightful share of the loot. It was not an ideal society, but it was one that respected the rights of the individual, regardless of his race, class, or religion.

In a world that was strictly organized by class and race, this was a revolutionary concept. Fifty years later, the founding fathers would take similar ideals and dress them in flowery language, giving birth to a new nation, dedicated to the pursuit of individual liberty.

While the number of pirates was not large and their reign was not long, these swashbuckling men have made an indelible impression on the popular imagination. Common sense tells us that pirates were nothing but thieves; our instincts tell us differently.

Although Daniel Collins' adventures are fictional, they are based on a story that is said to be true. The tale of Captain Scarfield's strange life is recorded by the great author and illustrator Howard Pyle.

Pyle obtained his information from two main sources: a report written by Lieutenant James Mainwaring preserved in the archives of the Royal Navy and a small chapbook published by Isaiah Thomas in 1821.

Some readers may be curious about the origins of the Man with the Silver Oar. This is no storyteller's invention, but a long-standing tradition in English law.

The silver oar was the mark of the authority of the Admiralty of the High Court. The ancient meaning of the symbol of the silver oar is lost to us, although ritual wooden oars, their blades painted silver, are still displayed in museums in England as remnants of this tradition.

I would like to thank those who provided visible and invisible support to this project. No author can do a book alone. Many people have contributed, in big and small ways.

Thanks to my editor, Ruth Katcher, who saw the promise of this book in its early stages and patiently navigated me through several drafts before it arrived in its present form.

Thanks to my agent, Liza Voges, for an endless stream of practical and moral support.

My writing partner, Dr. Barbara Baumgartner, provided insightful comments and much-needed historical research during the final months of the project. I will always be grateful for her willing ear and steady encouragement.

I wish to thank Bill Ward, Historical Director of the Philadelphia Seaport Museum, for help in searching out primary sources about maritime life in early America.

I also would like to take this opportunity to thank my wife, Jacqueline Moore, for her steadfast companionship and patience through the stormy waters of life.

I cannot forget to thank my children, Jesse and Rachel, who risked seasickness and sunstroke while their crazy dad learned to navigate a sailing ship during our research voyages to the Gulf of Mexico and the Caribbean Islands.

Maybe Daniel's story will inspire you to look more deeply into the nooks and crannies of our maritime history—perhaps that is where the real treasure still lies buried, for any of us to discover.

—ROBIN MOORE

FOR FURTHER READING

Bradlee, Francis. *Piracy in the West Indies and its Suppression*. Glorieta, New Mexico: Rio Grande Press, 1990.

Davis, Wade. *The Serpent and the Rainbow*. New York, NY: Warner Books, 1985.

Esquemeling, John. *The Buccaneers of America*. Glorieta, New Mexico: Rio Grande Press, 1992.

Gosse, Philip. *The History of Piracy*. Glorieta, New Mexico: Rio Grande Press, 1990.

Pyle, Howard. *Tales of Pirates and Buccaneers*. New York, NY: Random House, 1994.

Pyle, Howard. *The Buccaneers and Marooners of America*. Glorieta, New Mexico: Rio Grande Press, 1990.

Rediker, Marcus. *Between the Devil and the Deep Blue Sea*. New York: Cambridge University Press, 1987.

Verill, A. Hyatt. *In the Wake of the Buccaneers*. Glorieta, New Mexico: Rio Grande Press, 1990.

Verill, A. Hyatt. *The Real Story of the Pirate*. Glorieta, New Mexico: Rio Grande Press, 1989.

Williams, Robert. *Memoirs of a Buccaneer*. Glorieta, New Mexico: Rio Grande Press, 1990.

DATE DUE
